Helen Lacey grew up reading *Black Beauty* and *Little House on the Prairie*. These childhood classics inspired her to write her first book when she was seven, a story about a girl and her horse. She loves writing for Mills & Boon True Love, where she can create strong heroes with soft hearts and heroines with gumption who get their happily-ever-afters. For more about Helen, visit her website, www.helenlacey.com.

THE SECRET SON'S HOMECOMING

HELEN LACEY

MILLS & BOON

First Published in Great Britain 2018
by Mills & Boon, an imprint of HarperCollins*Publishers*
1 London Bridge Street, London, SE1 9GF

The Secret Son's Homecoming © 2018 Helen Lacey

ISBN: 978-0-263-26512-5

38-0718

MIX
Paper from
responsible sources
FSC C007454

For Robert

Who walks beside me
and catches my hand whenever I fall.

Chapter One

Connie Bedford knew from experience that regrets were pointless. She also knew that foolish behavior could not be undone—only not repeated. And she certainly had no intention of repeating the foolishness she'd carried out with the man standing across the dance floor from her.

Jonah Rickard.

Six feet plus of dark-haired, broad-shouldered, blue-eyed handsomeness that made her knees weak and turned her good sense to mush every time he was within a few feet of her.

Everyone had a weakness, she told herself. For some, it was chocolate or champagne. For others, it was extreme sports and adrenaline rushes. For Connie, it seemed as though it was Jonah. Even though she knew he was bad news and that he didn't appear to feel anything for her other than disdain.

And she didn't *like* him, either. Not really. It was simple chemistry. Alchemy. A straight-up physical reaction. The fact that it was still wreaking havoc with her good sense even though that crazy night had been over ten months ago frustrated her beyond belief. Particularly considering that every time she'd seen him since, each encounter had been even more awkward than the last. And it wasn't as though anything had *really* happened. Just a few minutes of insane impulsiveness. It should have been easy to forget.

I'm the master of forgetting things. I can forget this, too.

"Earth to Connie?"

She instantly turned on her heels. Nicola Radici stood behind her. Nicola O'Sullivan now, she corrected herself. And the very reason that Connie was at the O'Sullivan ranch. She'd had three weeks to help prepare her friend for the Cedar River wedding of the year, and she was delighted that the whole day had gone off without any drama. The tent, the tasteful decorations, the lighting, the electric fire pits keeping the cold early November air at bay—it was a dreamy and beautiful event. And Nicola looked amazing in her antique lace gown. Connie was thankful and happy that all the preparations had come together and the bride and groom had had a lovely ceremony. What didn't make her happy was the fact that Jonah was the groom's half brother, and since she was a bridesmaid, she knew she was about ten minutes away from being partnered with him on the dance floor.

Because the last thing in the world that she wanted was to be in his arms.

Again.

She shook off the memory of his touch suddenly seeping through her blood and tried to think about anything other than Jonah's arms, or any other part of him, for that matter. She half turned and faced the bride, plastering a smile on her face that was so sweet it made her teeth hurt.

"Sorry," she said to the smiling bride. "I'm in personal-assistant mode, just making sure everything's going off without a hitch."

Nicola, her beautiful face beaming, grasped Connie's arm. "You did an amazing job organizing everything so quickly. I can't thank you enough for making this happen."

"It wasn't all my doing," she said and grinned. "I'm a little OCD and like to be really organized. And you're my friend, so I wanted to do this."

"Today wouldn't have happened without you," Nicola assured her. "Now, have you seen my handsome husband?"

Connie curled her thumb toward the buffet table. "Over there."

Sure enough, Kieran O'Sullivan stood by the buffet, alongside his elder brother, Liam, his younger brother, Sean…and Jonah. Half brother to the three O'Sullivan siblings. Born out of a secret relationship their father, J. D. O'Sullivan, had with then-eighteen-year-old Kathleen Rickard. The whole situation was revealed when Liam, the eldest son, eloped with Kayla Rickard, Kathleen's niece. The Rickards and the O'Sullivans had been sworn enemies for thirty years—and Jonah was *the* secret spanning those decades. J.D. had, essentially, two separate families. One in Cedar River, South Dakota—the other in Portland, Oregon.

As Liam's personal assistant at the big O'Sullivan hotel in town, and a family friend, Connie had been privy to the entire situation for the past year. It was complicated and messy and had resulted in the end of J.D. and Gwen O'Sullivan's thirty-five-year marriage. But for the sake of their children and grandchildren, with some time and effort, the O'Sullivans and the Rickards had somehow managed to put aside their grievances and bitterness and tried to cobble together an uneasy truce from the fallout.

Well, except for Jonah.

He still clearly hated J.D. and resented the fact that his beloved mother had moved back to Cedar River so she could heal her estranged relationship with her own aging mother and brother. Yeah, *complicated* didn't cover the half of it. And it wasn't as though the O'Sullivan brothers hadn't tried to include Jonah in the reconciliation of the family—including J.D. It was just that Jonah was stubborn and his sole focus appeared to be protecting his mother—and resenting his father.

If she was a sensible woman—and she'd always considered herself to be—Connie knew she would put all thoughts of Jonah out of her mind and forget he existed. Like he had with her. Since he'd pretty much ignored her every time they'd met during the past ten months.

"They really are a good-looking bunch," Nicola said and grinned, gesturing toward the brothers, who were all dressed in dark gray suits with a flower at the lapel. "Don't you think?"

Connie managed an idle shrug. "Sure," she replied, thinking that they were all so handsome it was quite ridiculous. "An unfairly good gene pool."

As if on cue, Connie noticed, Kieran looked across the tent and made visual contact with his bride. The love between the newlyweds was palpable, and Connie experienced an acute sense of loneliness that made her heart ache. Which was silly, because she never considered herself to be *lonely*. She had a small circle of friends, and the O'Sullivans, of course, whom she cared for deeply and knew the feeling was reciprocated. But this was different. Nicola and Kieran were *in love*. Something Connie had never known, and considering her past, she wondered if she ever would. That kind of love imbued complete and utter trust in the other person—and Connie wasn't sure she'd ever be able to offer that to anyone. Or be vulnerable enough to accept it in return.

"I think I'm wanted," Nicola said on a sort of dreamy sigh before she gave Connie's arm a gentle squeeze and then floated across the dance floor.

Connie watched as the bride and groom met, just in time for the music to start. It was an old song, with lyrics about finding someone who made life worthwhile, and before long more members of the wedding party headed out to join them. Dread etched along every nerve she possessed, because Connie knew she was next. She brushed her hands down the long, deep purple–colored dress, made the pointless gesture of smoothing her hair in its perfect chignon and then took a step. And then another. And another.

It took exactly nine steps to reach him, and she experienced the same crazy rush of blood through her veins, the same heightened sense of awareness that being around him evoked. Never in her life had she reacted to anyone the way she reacted to him. And she didn't understand it. Why Jonah? He was aloof. He was indirectly disrespectful to the O'Sullivans. And he was a horse's ass. Sure, he was attractive and had incredible blue eyes…but she'd never been particularly drawn to good looks. And since he'd been unconscionably rude to her ten months earlier, she should have gotten over her infatuation, pronto.

She sucked in a breath, took another step and found herself meeting his gaze. Something flickered in his eyes, a kind of intense awareness that weakened her knees and amplified the knowledge that she really was the biggest fool of all time.

"Miss Bedford," he said and held out his hand.

Connie pressed her mouth together. He never used her first name. He kept the divide between them as wide as he could, and she assumed that focusing on her professional relationship with his family made it easier for him. He obviously didn't like her. Well, it was a mutual feeling.

Except…she didn't really want to be that way with Jonah. No, what she felt toward him was something else. Something she didn't quite have the courage to acknowledge.

She experienced a quiver across her skin as their fingertips connected, and then his hand closed over hers and he drew her closer. The cologne he wore was subtle and masculine and assailed her senses instantly, latching onto her memory like a narcotic. And suddenly she was back inside his hotel room, back feeling his hands roam across her skin, experiencing the possession of his mouth on hers. She'd been all too ready to get lost in the moment of passion… Until another memory had kicked in, one that had a familiar and polarizing effect right to her core.

His grip tightened fractionally, as though he'd recognized she was on the verge of flight mode.

"Relax," he said quietly, moving one arm around her waist. "It's just a dance."

Connie swallowed hard, ignored her pounding heart and told herself he was right. It *was* just a dance. And it would soon be over. He'd release her. She'd be free to scurry back to the sidelines where she could forget all about her crazy overreaction to Jonah Rickard.

She stepped on his foot and wobbled. "Sorry."

"Don't worry about it," he said blandly, his hold around her waist firm but unthreatening.

Her eyes barely reached his chin, even in her heels,

and she curled one hand over his shoulder, balancing herself. "I'm not much of a dancer."

"I noticed."

One thing about Jonah Rickard—he could make any remark sound like an insult without so much as batting an eyelid. "I wasn't sure you'd be here," she said, aiming for a dig.

His shoulders tensed fractionally. "It's my half brother's wedding."

He always said *half brother*. He would never acknowledge the O'Sullivans as anything other than an unwanted part of his DNA.

"You didn't RSVP," she said, one brow up, trying to keep her feet moving to the ridiculously romantic song playing in the background. "For yourself or a guest."

He made a soft scoffing sound. "Is that a roundabout way of asking if I'm seeing anyone at the moment?"

Color seeped up her neck, and she gritted her back teeth. "Certainly not. It's just polite to let people know these things…that is, if you actually care about other people."

His jaw tightened. "I told Kieran I'd be a groomsman. I didn't realize that came with a contractual obligation." He glanced at his watch and his mouth twitched. "Two whole minutes and we're already on the verge of an argument… That might be a record, Miss Bedford."

"Would you stop calling me that?"

"No."

Irritation coursed across her skin.

"You're such a jerk. I can't believe I almost…"

Her words trailed off as shame and humiliation found its way into her blood and then took root through to her bones. The song changed and Connie thought it was her chance to escape, to pull free of his embrace and leave him standing in the middle of the dance floor. The more she considered it, the more she realized that his hold on her had loosened and he was almost inviting her to bail.

"I don't think either of us needs a trip down memory lane," he said, low into her ear, almost in a whisper. "Do we?"

"Coming to my senses before it was too late was the smartest thing I've ever done," she snapped tightly.

"Is that what you did?" he inquired, his voice so soft she felt herself lean closer so she could hear him.

"Yes. But I…"

"You…what?" he queried when her words trailed off.

Connie quickly recalled everything that had transpired that night. She'd willingly gone to his room. She'd willingly responded to his kisses. And then she'd changed her mind. In his defense, he'd done nothing dishonorable. He'd hadn't tried to sway her or convince her to betray her principles with words or actions or made her feel threatened in any way. She'd said no, and he'd accepted it. Even so, he clearly still resented her for rejecting him.

In hindsight, she couldn't believe she'd behaved in such an out-of-character fashion. She didn't do hotel rooms or spend the night with guys she hardly knew. At the time she'd only met him on a couple of occasions. It had been his first visit to Cedar River, the first time he'd met his extended family. She worked for his brother and should have steered clear of him for obvious reasons. Muddying waters wasn't her thing. Complicated wasn't her thing. Neither was drama. She'd had enough of that in the past to last her a lifetime.

"I didn't mean to lead you on," she said softly.

He shrugged loosely. "It doesn't matter now. Let's just keep ignoring one another. For the sake of harmony, it's probably better that way."

Then he released her, turned on his heel and walked off, leaving her standing in the center of the dance floor and realizing that he'd done exactly what she'd wanted to do to him.

Jonah wasn't sure what it was about Connie Bedford that pushed his buttons so much.

But she did.

Big time.

And it wasn't only about that night ten months earlier. Sure, she'd dented his ego. There was something about her that got under his skin. And no one, *ever*, did that. He'd spent his life keeping pretty much everyone— except his mother—at a figurative arm's length. It made it easier to hold on to resentment, to hate his father and remain cautious about getting too close to his newfound half siblings. Now he had family everywhere he looked— a grandmother, an uncle, a cousin, nieces and nephews... the list appeared to keep on growing. And now that Kieran was married to Nicola, no doubt there would be more babies on the way in the future.

Having to fake a familial connection with so many people was exhausting. So he didn't waste energy doing it. Which meant everyone thought he was arrogant and unlikable. And maybe he was. But he didn't have anything to prove, and all he cared about was ensuring his mom was safe and happy. *She* was his family. Not these strangers who looked so much like him.

Because that's what they were. Strangers. His life was filled with them. Each one trying to take a piece of him, trying to make him *fit in*. The truth was, fitting in with them didn't interest him. He wasn't and never would be an O'Sullivan. He didn't need J.D.'s last name, his money or the legacy that came with both of those things. He only wanted his mother to be happy, and since she'd decided to move back to Cedar River, a small town in the shadow of the Black Hills, he found himself commuting from Portland more often than he liked. Something he'd do until he was sure his mother was settled and happy. He stayed at Kieran's old apartment and minded his own business, unless he was forced to hang out with his half brothers.

He'd become used to them interfering over the past few months—particularly Liam and Kieran, since Sean lived in California and rarely made it back to Cedar River. The older O'Sullivan siblings seemed to have made inclusion part of their DNA. And it irritated the hell out of him. Jonah didn't want to be a part of their family. He had enough going on working out a way to fit in with the Rickards.

And to top it off, there was Connie. Blond hair, gray eyes, curves in all the right places. Liam's personal assistant, a family friend and so far under his skin he couldn't bear to be in the same room as her. She had him under some kind of crazy, lustful spell, and he acted like a jerk every time they were together.

Of course, it was just sex.

He wanted to get her into bed.

End of story.

Their aborted make-out session had stupidly only amplified his desire for her. Of course, she had every right to change her mind, but he couldn't help thinking that she'd become spooked in some way and that's why she'd put the brakes on and then fled. He had no idea what he'd done to make her react that way because she'd left his room without an explanation. Now they couldn't share a few words of conversation without it becoming a resentment-fueled disagreement. Not that he wanted to get cozy and friendly with Connie Bedford. He didn't do that with anyone. But he had enough going on without the added aggravation of a certain blonde bombarding his thoughts every time he came to visit his mom. And it didn't help that everyone named O'Sullivan seemed to think of her as some kind of angel incarnate. Connie did things. Connie fixed things. Connie had pretty much organized Kieran's wedding single-handedly. Connie was the go-to girl. The person everyone leaned on to get things done. And she did it without complaint, so perhaps she *was* an angel. Because in his experience, no human being was that altruistic.

Maybe she had an endgame? Some kind of motive for being on call for the O'Sullivans 24/7. Not that it was any of his business. Connie Bedford could do what she liked, with whomever she liked, whenever she liked.

"Having a good time?"

Liam.

Jonah recognized his half brother's voice immediately. Other than J.D., the man was his least favorite O'Sullivan. But Liam was the one who never let up—who acted like a *big brother* whenever he had the opportunity. And he monopolized most of Connie's time and attention, since she'd been his personal assistant at the hotel for the past five years. Jonah wasn't sure why it bugged him…but it did.

"Yeah, sure," he replied and grabbed a wineglass from one of the passing waiters. "You know how much I love a good family gathering."

Liam laughed. "God, you're obnoxious."

"One of my finer qualities."

His brother shook his head. "Have you spoken to Dad this weekend?"

Jonah took a drink, ignored the awful sweetness of the wine and shrugged. "I've been busy."

"You said you'd make an effort if we backed off and let you do this at your own pace," Liam reminded him.

"I know what I said," Jonah replied, spying Connie across the tent and hating that he was still thinking about her. "And I will."

"It's Thanksgiving in a couple of weeks," Liam said. "It would be nice if you were there for him. Kayla's folks and grandmother are coming to our place for dinner. So are my mother and Kieran and Nicola and the boys. And Liz's girls will be there for some of the day."

Liz, his half sister, had died a few years earlier. Jonah had heard the story many times. She'd left behind three young daughters and a rancher husband who had since remarried. The family was clearly still grieving, but given his own issues with the family, Jonah didn't know how to feel about it.

"What do you expect me to say?" he asked his half brother.

Liam frowned. "All I'm saying is that I think Dad will be at loose ends."

"I generally spend the holidays with my mom," he said flatly. "I can't see this year being any different."

"We invited your mother," Liam told him, so matter-of-fact it sounded like the most obvious thing in the world. "She declined, considering *my* mother would be there. So, I thought maybe Dad could—"

"I don't want J.D. hanging around my mom," Jonah said quickly, feeling rage rise through his blood. "Ever."

Liam's mouth twitched. "You might not have a say in the matter."

"What the hell does that mean?"

"It means," his brother said and tapped him on the shoulder, "that as much as you want to, you don't get to tell anyone how to live their life. Including and especially your parents. Now, be a big boy and go and talk to Dad."

Dad...

Jonah hadn't called J. D. O'Sullivan that since he was five years old.

And he never would again. He didn't consider J.D. to be his father. He was the man who'd impregnated his mother when she was eighteen years old. End of story. There was no nice way around it. The fact that J.D. hadn't technically abandoned his mom or him didn't make one iota of difference. As far as Jonah was concerned, he didn't have a father and was quite happy to keep it that way.

As if on cue, he spotted J.D. in the crowd, deep in discussion with people he knew were friends of the bride and groom. He also spotted Liam's mother, Gwen O'Sullivan, a few feet away, clearly keeping a respectable distance between herself and her ex-husband. He admired her poise and elegance and the way she'd dropped J.D. like a hot coal once she'd discovered his lies and infidelity. Jonah had met her several times, and despite expecting her to treat him with disdain and resentment, Gwen was always polite and appeared to harbor no bad feelings toward him. He'd even attended her recent birthday celebration, albeit very briefly, as a gesture of respect.

Tired of the conversation with his half brother, Jonah waved a dismissive hand and headed inside the house. The O'Sullivan ranch was the largest around, and the house looked as though it could have been on the cover of a style magazine. The O'Sullivans were third-generation money and the wealthiest family in Cedar River. But money had never impressed Jonah, even though J.D. had showered him with extravagant gifts when he was younger. Bikes, electronic equipment, even a brand-new

Jeep when he got his learner's permit. None of it had made a lick of difference. What he'd wanted back then had nothing to do with the expensive gifts that felt like a payoff.

Family.

A mom and dad and maybe a couple of siblings. Instead, there was J.D.—turning up every few months, full of excuses and handouts and time frames. A couple of days here and there, the occasional birthday, graduation… whenever he could fit them in between his real family. With postscripts about his other children. Jonah had been raised on a steady diet of tales about his half siblings and Cedar River and life on the big O'Sullivan ranch. And through all those years, they knew nothing about him. He was a guilty secret. A side note to his father's perfect life. Until Liam had eloped with Kayla Rickard and everything had been blown out of the water in spectacular fashion.

Now, he was a part of them, drawn into their lives without his consent and feeling resistance with every fiber he possessed. Tied by blood but always the outsider, destined to be the illegitimate and unwanted son of J. D. O'Sullivan.

He shook off his thoughts and headed down the hallway and into the front living room. He'd been inside the house a couple of times, and since Gwen had decided she wanted to get a place in town and Kieran and his new bride planned on moving in, he figured his invitations would soon become more frequent. Nicola had custody of her two orphaned nephews, and Jonah had to admit the ranch would be a great place for the kids to grow up.

Jonah came to a halt in the doorway, spotting Connie by the window. She was staring out, clearly looking for some time alone. He was about to turn and leave when she said his name and turned slightly.

"I didn't mean to disturb you," he said quickly. "I was looking for some—"

"Downtime?" she suggested, cutting him off. "Me, too. Don't get me wrong, I love weddings, but once everything is done and the bride and groom are relaxed and happy, I always seem to need a little time-out."

He took a couple of steps into the room. "How many of these things have you helped organize?"

Her mouth twisted in a smile. "A few."

Jonah let out a breath and took another step. "Don't you ever get tired of it?"

"Tired of what?"

"Doing things for everyone else."

She turned fully to face him, and he was struck by how effortlessly beautiful she was. Even with her tightly coiffed hair, purple dress and perfect makeup...there was a naturalness about her that affected him on a kind of primal level. He tried to ignore it, tried to deny it—but there was no denying the truth. He was hot for Connie Bedford. Raging hot. And he didn't know what the hell to do about it. He'd never been at the mercy of his libido before.

"I've always considered it a privilege to do things for others."

He laughed humorlessly. "God, you're naive."

"Because I like to help people?"

"Because you let people walk all over you."

She moved, taking a couple of long strides. "Like who?"

"Liam," he said pointedly.

"He's my employer," she shot back.

"Didn't you look after his kid last night?" Jonah reminded her. "Is babysitting in your job description, too?"

"They had trouble finding a replacement sitter on short notice and the whole family was at the rehearsal dinner."

"I know," he said and moved to stand behind the couch, watching her, fascinated as her cheeks scorched with color. "I was there."

"So, you know the whole story."

"I know my brother takes advantage of you. I know you pick up J.D.'s dry cleaning. I know you do errands for Gwen O'Sullivan."

She moved closer, until there was only the sofa between them, her chest heaving. Jonah tried his best not to stare, but she was damned impossible to ignore. He'd had his fair share of relationships and lovers, but he couldn't ever remember wanting a woman the way he wanted Connie.

"Obviously you've never done an *unselfish* thing in your life."

"It's not unselfish to refuse to become someone's doormat," he offered.

Her hands jerked to her hips in dramatic fashion. "I think that's the most insulting thing anyone has ever said to me."

"Then you've lived a sheltered life."

"I'd rather that than be mean-spirited and unpleasant. I can't believe you're actually related to the O'Sullivans."

Jonah rocked back a little on his heels. "You're not the only one."

"You're not fit to wipe their boots."

Irritation kerneled in his chest and Jonah was suddenly all out of patience. Her blind faith in the O'Sullivans was astounding. "No need to...not when you're at their beck and call day and night."

She glared at him. "I don't know how I ever...ever..."

Her words trailed off. "How you what?" he shot back.

"Ended up in my hotel room with your tongue in my mouth and—"

"You're such a jerk," she said, cutting him off. "How do you sleep at night?"

He raised a brow. "If you'd stayed in my bed that night, you would have found out."

Chapter Two

Connie shook her head. "You're such a conceited ass. Bailing was the smartest thing I've ever done."

He scowled, clearly not liking the fact that she was laughing at him. "Speaking the truth doesn't make me conceited, Con—" He stopped and she knew he fought hard to check himself. "I mean, Miss Bedford. Your dedication to the O'Sullivans might seem honorable, but it also makes me wonder *why*. Money doesn't appear to be your motive. Or power, since you've worked for Liam for five years and the old man before that. I don't know… maybe you're infatuated with one of them."

Connie took a moment to absorb his words. And then she laughed. "Really? That's your theory on my loyalty?"

He shrugged, then tugged at his collar. "It makes sense. You and Liam spend a lot of time together," he said quietly. "It explains your devotion and utter compliance to everything he says and does."

If she didn't know better, she could have sworn that he was actually jealous. But that made no sense. They were nothing to one another. "Beside the fact that he's married and that Kayla and your brother are very happy together, Liam is my boss. And my friend. But since you probably don't have any friends, I wouldn't expect you to understand."

Now *he* laughed, a soft, deeply resonant chuckle that affected her deep down. She hated that he could do that. In fact, she despised everything about him, deciding that sexual attraction *definitely* had nothing to do with actually liking someone.

"Have I pushed a button?"

"I wouldn't let you close enough to push my buttons."

"Now, we both know that's not entirely true," he said quietly, his dark hair shining beneath the light, his blue eyes glittering brilliantly.

"You're insufferable," she said in a huff. "If you must know, that night was completely out of character for me. I'd had a bad day and decided to have a drink after work. I didn't expect to see you at the bar. And then one thing led to another and…well…you know the rest."

"You mean the part where you sprinted to my room?"

Heat infused her cheeks. "I would hardly call it a sprint. Anyway, you weren't exactly difficult to convince."

"I thought a beautiful woman wanted me to make love to her," he said quietly, his voice as seductive as a caress. "I'm not made of stone, despite what you may think."

All Connie could think was the fact that he'd just said she was beautiful. The words rattled around in her head with the deafening power of a freight train. She'd never considered herself beautiful. Well groomed, maybe, with nice hair and an average build…but knowing Jonah thought she was beautiful made her belly roll over and over.

"I don't think you're made of stone," she said and shrugged. "It's only that sometimes you can be so…so infuriating."

"Part of my charm."

"You're *not* charming," she assured him.

"Not like Liam, eh?"

She made an impatient sound. "Would you stop inferring that I have feelings for your brother? Because I don't."

"Prove it," he challenged. "Criticize him."

She scowled. "I'm not going to play stupid games to help inflate your ego."

"My ego is rock solid," he said. "It needs to be around you, Miss Bedford."

Connie didn't miss the insinuation—or his return to formality. "If it's any consolation, it wouldn't have mattered whose room I was in that night…the outcome would have been the same. I'm only thankful that it was someone as rational and considerate as you. I guess it could have ended very differently if I'd been with someone else."

His gaze narrowed. "Is that a compliment?"

She shrugged. "An observation."

"No means no," he said quietly. "Always. There are no half measures when it comes to a person's choice about who they sleep with."

Connie's suspicions were confirmed. Despite the rude way he'd dismissed her that night, he had integrity. *No means no.* Such a simple statement had more meaning to her than he could ever understand.

"I don't sleep around. I don't have one-night stands. I'm a boring, stay-at-home girl who likes to read romantic novels and curl up on the couch with my dogs."

"I figured you'd be a cat person."

She relaxed a fraction. "Nope. Four dogs. And a gold-fish."

"No boyfriend?"

"No," she replied, stunned that he'd asked her some-thing so personal. "You?"

His mouth twisted. "I like girls."

Connie chuckled. "I meant, no girlfriend?"

"Haven't we established that I came to this wedding stag? Remember how I forgot to RSVP?"

"I thought you did that simply to stick it to the O'Sullivans," she suggested. "You know, to prove that they don't own you."

His mouth curled at the edges. "I really do have a bad reputation."

"Yes," she said. "You do."

"You know, Connie, I'm not all bad."

The way he unexpectedly said her name again made her toes curl. He had seduction imprinted in his DNA, she was certain. "Time will tell, I suppose. And I really need to get back to the party."

"Hoping to catch the bouquet?"

Her breath hiked up. "No. Have to give the band their final payment."

"So, doing O'Sullivan bidding right until the end?"

Her temper quickly returned. "Doing my job. See you later. Or not at all. Either would suit me just fine."

By the time she made it back down the hallway, Con-nie had slowed down her breathing and calmed her nerves. Other than that crazy night, it was the longest and most in-depth conversation she'd had with him in ten months. He tried so hard not to fit in with his fam-ily, when the truth was that he was actually more like them than he'd ever admit. Particularly Liam and J.D., who were both confident and self-assured and strong.

Jonah possessed those qualities in spades. And something else…an aura of *don't mess with me* arrogance that, rather than having her running for hills, was sexy and thrilling and somehow a powerful turn-on. She secretly liked that about him, that he didn't roll over and do what was expected. While her allegiance would always be with the O'Sullivans, she admired his determination *not to* take the easy route and try to fit in without complaint. Of course, her feelings were illogical. He openly resisted getting close to his family and her loyalty to them made it impossible for her to excuse his behavior.

But her dreams were a different story. In them, she could want him without explanation. She could watch as he slew dragons with his indifference and determination to remain aloof and apart from the people with whom she shared blood and birthright.

I've read way too many romantic novels.

But didn't every woman have the right to fall for a Heathcliff every now and then?

It wasn't as though he was marriage material. It was a fantasy. A secret longing for a man who possessed brooding sexiness in abundance, and probably had ice water in his veins. And Connie tended to doubt she'd ever get married, anyhow. Maybe marriage wasn't in her makeup. She'd become a career woman through necessity and felt safe in her cocoon of work, home, friends…and the O'Sullivans. Working at the hotel since she was sixteen had shaped her path; being Liam's assistant for the past five years and working for J.D. before that had given her purpose and strength and empowerment—everything she'd so desperately needed. Jonah was wrong—she wasn't a doormat. She did everything with a measure of control and commitment, obliging others because that was her *choice*.

My choice to say yes.

My choice to say no.

Survivor's code, ingrained into the very fiber of her soul. Without it, she would have frayed at the seams until there was nothing left of who she'd been before that terrible day when her life had irrevocably changed.

"What are you doing, hiding out in here?"

Connie swiveled on her heels, realizing she'd ended up in the kitchen and that J. D. O'Sullivan was hanging out behind the countertop, drinking what appeared to be antacid. A lot of people considered him to be loud and blustery and arrogant—and perhaps he was—but Connie also knew he was compassionate and generous and kind, even if he didn't always allow the world to see it. He had a reputation for speaking his mind and had no tolerance for fools. *The apple doesn't fall far from the tree.* Yes, Jonah Rickard was more like his father than he would ever willingly admit.

"I could ask you the same thing," she said and winked.

"Damn ulcer is acting up," he admitted and held up the glass. "I thought this might help."

It occurred to her that it probably wasn't something he'd openly acknowledge, but Connie had arranged for more than one specialist appointment for J.D. over the years.

"Spicy food, stress and alcohol," she reminded him. "You know the drill…they're all off the menu."

He shrugged his giant shoulders. "Well, the food and booze I can easily give up. The stress is the hard one."

"I don't imagine being back in this house is helping," she offered gently, recalling how he'd been kicked out of the ranch by his very angry wife over ten months earlier. Now he lived permanently at the hotel, despite both Liam and Kieran offering to have him come live with them. But Connie knew J.D. was too proud and stubborn to hang on to the fringes of his son's lives. "I know Kieran is happy you are here today."

"I wouldn't let my son down," he said and then smiled ruefully. "I've done enough of that lately."

"Kieran has a big capacity for forgiveness. So does Liam," she added gently.

"But not Sean and Jonah," he said. "Right?"

Connie half shrugged. "I don't know either of them as well," she replied and figured it was the truth. Sean had lived in Los Angeles for over a decade, and Jonah was, well...*Jonah*. "But I'm sure they'll all come around."

"Maybe Sean," he said hopefully. "Jonah, however, is another story altogether."

"I'm sure he's not as difficult as he makes out."

J.D. laughed and it crinkled the corners of his eyes. "Ha, you've met my youngest son, right?"

Met him. Touched him. Kissed him. Dreamed of him.

Connie swallowed hard. "Sometimes people say and do things they don't mean to cover up how they really feel, and so they don't appear vulnerable. Perhaps that's it. Maybe he's afraid to show you how he really feels."

"I know how he really feels," J.D. said and winced. "He hates me."

"I'm sure he doesn't."

"He does," J.D. said. "And there's nothing I can do about it."

"You're right about that."

Jonah.

Connie turned her head and saw him standing in the doorway. She noticed that J.D.'s broad shoulders sagged slightly and saw sadness in the older man's expression. There was nothing but resentment and bitterness emanating from Jonah, and it was aimed directly at his father.

And at her.

* * *

Jonah was so furious he couldn't stand being in his own skin. J.D. and Connie, talking about him in hushed voices behind his back as though it was everyday conversation. And maybe it was. Maybe he was the usual topic of conversation for the whole damned family, or the whole damned town!

But that didn't mean he had to like it, or allow it. J.D. had done enough damage over the years.

"Have you both finished dissecting me?" he demanded.

"We were just—"

"I know what you were doing," he shot back, glaring at the other man, not daring to look toward Connie. "And I want it to stop."

The silence was suddenly deafening. Every time he was near J.D., his resentment fired up; every time he thought about the man who'd so recklessly become involved with his mother, Jonah experienced an acute sense of loathing and rage. It never abated, not in all the years since he was old enough to understand the situation. Kathleen had left Cedar River—left her family—so she could have her baby in secret and not blow the O'Sullivan empire apart. He understood his mother's motives, and he respected them, but he hated J.D. and everything he stood for—his dishonesty, his betrayal, his lack of integrity and honor—and vowed he would never demonstrate those qualities. Vowed to become a better man than J. D. O'Sullivan.

"Jonah, I think your dad just meant that—"

"Don't call him that," he growled, meeting her gaze for the first time since he'd entered the room. She blanched, and he registered a sharp feeling of guilt somewhere through the haze that was his rage. "This situation has nothing to do with you… It's about him and me and my mother. Please stay out of it."

"I can't do that," she said and he watched as her throat rolled over convulsively. "I care too much about your family and I won't see them hurt…not by anyone."

"Connie," J.D. said quickly. "It's okay. Don't worry about it."

"That's good advice," Jonah shot back and glared at Connie, suddenly mesmerized by the way she glared back, not giving an inch. "You should take it."

She took a long breath. "You know something," she said quietly, her chin held at a tight angle. "You really don't deserve them."

It was a deliberate and cutting remark. Then she said goodbye to J.D. and left the room, ignoring Jonah completely. But he felt damned by the trace of her perfume that floated past him as she disappeared through the doorway. Jonah cursed his own stupidity before turning to glare at the other man in the room.

"She's quite a girl," J.D. said and half smiled. "Don't you think?"

"I'd rather not speculate."

"That's reassuring," he replied. "She's a nice young woman and shouldn't be messed with."

Jonah almost laughed out loud. "I have no intention of *messing* with Miss Bedford," he said, ignoring the twitch in his stomach. "She's way too invested in your family. Actually, I'm not sure if it's you or Liam that she's infatuated with."

J.D. laughed. "Don't be ridiculous. Liam's happily married and I'm old enough to be her father."

"We all know your weakness for younger women."

The older man's smile disappeared. "I was thirty-one

when I fell in love with your mother. She was eighteen. That's not exactly a lifetime between us."

Jonah wanted to cover his ears. He'd heard the story countless times. J.D. had fallen for Kathleen. They had an affair. She got pregnant. J.D. wanted to come clean and admit to his adultery, but Kathleen had persuaded him to remain in Cedar River and stay with his family while she gave up everything…for him.

Yeah, he knew the story…knew his mother, too, had made her choices over the years. But he still blamed J.D. entirely for taking advantage of a much younger woman.

"I don't want to have this conversation again," Jonah said quietly, harnessing his emotions as best he could.

"At this stage, I'll take any conversation I can get."

Jonah scowled. "Why the hell would you want to?"

"Because you're my son."

He winced. "You know I'm not interested in being anything to you."

J.D. nodded. "I know."

"But you still keep coming back for more of the same?" He shook his head. "I don't understand it."

J.D. placed his big hands on the counter. "Well, I'm hoping that one day, you just might."

Jonah ignored the odd sensation suddenly seeping through his blood. He didn't want to spend time with J.D. He didn't want to waste time listening to platitudes about fathers and sons.

"I've gotta go," he said and fished his car keys from his pocket, thinking he'd had just about enough wedding nonsense and happy *family* time for one day. He needed the solitude of his apartment. Well, technically it was Kieran's apartment, but he'd been bunking there off and on since his mother had moved back to Cedar River. Sometimes he stayed at the hotel, but with J.D. now in residence there, the less time he spent at O'Sullivans, the better.

Jonah left the room and headed outside. He offered a quick goodbye to the bride and groom, knowing it was bad form to leave the ceremony before they did, and tried to shake off the guilt he felt as he drove home. The huge Victorian house, which had been split into several apartments, greeted him with the kind of quiet, uncomplicated seclusion he favored. Okay…so maybe that was a stretch. It wasn't as though he *longed* for his own company. He'd always had a circle of friends and coworkers and socialized as much as the next person. In Portland he still had a few close friends from college and enjoyed their company. But regularly visiting South Dakota had been a no-brainer. He wasn't about to let his mother wade through her past without him close at hand. She needed him. He had a spacious and modern apartment in Portland, a vast contrast with the old-fashioned Victorian, with its shuttered windows and mix of old and new furnishings. Before Kieran had leased the place, it had been Kayla's home. Sometimes he felt stifled by the familial connection to the apartment, but it was convenient and the rent was reasonable.

Once he got home, Jonah ditched the suit, took a shower, changed into jeans, a sweater and lined jacket, pulled on his boots, made coffee and headed outside onto the small terrace. Tomorrow was Sunday and he planned on visiting his mother, but before that he had to drop by the hotel to catch up with Liam about the proposed extension plans for the local museum and art gallery. Kayla was the curator and Liam had provided most of the funding for the council-approved extension. Jonah knew he'd been offered the contract to solidify the family connection… but it was good business and he was no fool.

Once he finished the coffee, Jonah went back inside, grabbed a beer from the fridge and slumped onto the sofa. He grabbed the remote, flicked through a few channels and settled on a NASCAR event. The mindless drone of engines relaxed him and he settled back, perched his feet on the coffee table and dropped his head back and closed his eyes. He had the vague thought that he was done with weddings for a while. He'd never had any interest in getting married himself—at least, not yet. He'd never had a long-term relationship—no doubt a hang-up from his father's lack of commitment to his wife and the double life he'd led for the past thirty years.

When he woke up it was two in the morning. He had a crick in his neck, the beer was untouched on the table and the neighbor's cat was curled up on the sofa beside him. The damned feline often sneaked in and made himself comfortable on Jonah's sofa, bed or lap. He belonged to the elderly woman in the downstairs apartment and was notorious for getting into trouble. Jonah had already rescued the cat twice when he'd gotten caught on top of the gazebo in the backyard.

Jonah got up, stretched out his limbs and then headed to bed. When he finally awoke it was past eight and he drank two cups of strong coffee to clear the fuzziness in his head, a feeling he blamed on the half a glass of celebratory wine he'd sipped at the reception and the resentment still churning in his gut. He dressed, made toast he didn't eat and then headed into town.

Sunday mornings in Cedar River were quiet, except for the tourists milling at the few open coffeehouses and the bakery on Main Street. Of course, the hotel was open, and he pulled into a reserved space next to his brother's recognizable Silverado. He drove a sedan when he was in town, mostly to annoy J.D., who insisted he needed an SUV and kept offering to buy him one to replace the Jeep Jonah had sold the minute he'd started college. Jonah headed for the main doors and the concierge greeted him by name. His connection to the O'Sullivan family was known around town and he couldn't deny it at the hotel. Still, as he walked through the place, he experienced a familiar and acute sense of dishonor about who and what he was. It was J.D.'s shame, but in Cedar River, he always felt as though he wore it like a cattle brand.

The hotel was impressive and luxurious and as good as any found in a large city. It employed dozens of locals and the service was exemplary, no doubt due to Liam being at the helm. Apparently he'd turned the place around in the last five years, developing it into a true boutique destination, and it was hard not to admire his half brother's business acumen.

Jonah strode across the lobby and caught the elevator to the third floor and the private suite of offices. He used his swipe card to reach the top floor. Liam's office took up a significant section, plus there were several suites kept available for family and a few corporate offices and a conference room.

He walked through the front office and spotted Connie sitting at her desk, her head bent, her fingers flicking quickly over the computer keyboard.

"It's Sunday," he said and stopped. "Since when do you work on Sunday?"

She looked up, her face expressionless, and clearly expecting to see him. "Liam had to step out for a bit. He'll be back in about twenty minutes." She got up and came around the desk, a folder in her hands. "He asked if you could look over this while you wait. You can go into his office."

Jonah stayed where he was. She wore jeans and a

bright red shirt, tucked in at the waist, with a sparkly belt and bright blue cowboy boots. Her hair was down, moving over her shoulders as she walked, and it struck him that this was the first time he'd seen her with her hair that way. It was always up in a professional braid or like the fancy style she'd had at the wedding. And the clothes... He'd only ever seen her in her corporate suit and jacket or an evening dress. But today she looked casual and young and more beautiful than he'd ever seen her before. Her face was free of makeup and he spotted a row of freckles across the bridge of her nose.

Damn. *Freckles.* Something kerneled in his chest, a heavy feeling he didn't like, and he realized what it was. Attraction. But since she was regarding him with contempt and undisguised impatience, Jonah also felt like a first-rate fool.

She'd made her thoughts abundantly clear that night ten months ago. He'd been at the bar downstairs, looking for solace and a way to purge the rage pounding through his blood. She'd been alone at a booth, staring into a club soda. He knew who she was. He'd met her that first time he'd accompanied his mother to Cedar River when she'd returned to see her family after thirty years away from the small town. Liam's secret marriage to Kayla had been the catalyst for Kathleen's return, and Jonah wasn't about to allow her to face everyone without him. What he hadn't bargained on was Connie Bedford. He had recognized an instant attraction.

Jonah knew enough about women to home in on sexual chemistry. So, that night, they'd talked for a while. And when the talking stopped and they both clearly knew where things were heading, he invited her to his room and she agreed. Outside, before he could pull the key card from his wallet, she'd leaned in toward him and he'd kissed her. Softly at first, because her lips had been so damned inviting he'd wanted to savor every moment. And then desire took over and he kissed her with so much passion it had almost dropped him to his knees. Within minutes they were in his room and on his bed. It had been hot and heavy, and he couldn't remember a time when he'd wanted a woman so much—until she put the brakes on, which had acted like a bucket of ice water on his libido.

Of course, he'd stopped, immediately. But he'd also been wound up and frustrated by his inability to get her to confide in him when something was so obviously bothering her. He wasn't usually *that* guy. Sure, his relationships had always been casual, but he always treated women with respect and restraint and courtesy.

Until Connie Bedford.

He'd been rude and unpleasant, stung less by her sudden rejection than the lack of explanation, and his manners hadn't improved since. She was under his skin. Being around her pushed *all* his buttons…physical and emotional. He couldn't explain or understand it, since they barely knew one another. But he knew she disapproved of his behavior and his feelings toward the O'Sullivans, and the fact that she kindled that spark of shame within him when even his mother couldn't irritated him down to the very blood in his bones.

Jonah took the folder and noticed that Connie seemed… uncomfortable. Her gaze kept slipping toward the door, almost as though… "Am I making you nervous?"

Her gaze jerked upward. "Of course not."

"You seem nervous being alone with me. You keep looking to see if your boss is coming."

"Caffeine withdrawal," she said and crossed her arms. "I'm trying to give up coffee, but I can smell it from the kitchen." She was so clearly lying to him—and he was instantly compelled to try to put her at ease.

"Why would you want to do that?" he inquired. "Coffee is one of life's guilty pleasures."

"My goal is to give up all the things that are bad for me. Coffee is on the list."

"What else is on your list?" he asked, picking up the scent of her flowery perfume and feeling it spike through his blood like wildfire.

"You."

He laughed, both aroused and amused by her candor. "I don't think I've ever been on a list before."

"Ten bucks says you have."

He laughed again and realized he did that a lot around Connie. She was so effortlessly attractive, and he pushed back the urge to reach out and touch her hair, her cheek. It wouldn't be appropriate, considering their history. They might have chemistry, but it was so much more than that because something about her affected him on a primal level. He couldn't work it out. Sure, she was pretty, but there was an earnestness about Connie that was refreshing and intoxicating and made him—foolishly—want to get to know her better. Somehow, she made him think that she'd be a good friend. Which was crazy, because he had several female friends back in Portland and he didn't want to take any of *them* to bed.

"Why are you really working today?" he asked.

She shrugged and moved back around the desk. "Just catching up on a few things."

"And you still don't think they take advantage of you?"

Her mouth thinned. "Maybe I'm one of those people who like being needed. You should try it sometime... doing something for someone without a motive."

Her dig had pinpoint accuracy. "I'm not completely selfish."

"If you weren't you'd know that every time you call your father J.D. it hurts his feelings terribly."

Jonah stiffened. "I have my reasons."

"Yes," she agreed. "Selfish ones."

"You don't know anything about it."

"Actually," she corrected, "I know quite a bit. We doormats tend to hear everyone's tale of woe."

Jonah's stomach rolled. "I shouldn't have called you that. I'm sorry."

"Wow, an apology. I bet that makes your teeth hurt."

"A bit," he admitted. "But I generally don't have to apologize for my behavior, since my behavior is usually very civilized."

"Are you saying I bring out the worst in you?"

"You bring out something," he admitted rawly. "But I'm not quite sure what it is. I think I find your complete and utter faith in the O'Sullivans a mystery. And damned irritating."

"Haven't you ever looked up to and admired someone?"

"Of course," he replied. "My mom. My best friend from high school. My favorite professor in college. Your point?"

"That it's not *blind* faith," she replied. "It's respect and admiration. It's knowing someone has your back and you have theirs. It's about friendship and loyalty."

"And your loyalty lies with Liam and J.D.?" he probed. "Why?"

"Because they saved my life."

Chapter Three

Connie wanted to snatch the words back the moment they left her mouth. Having a heart-to-heart with Jonah wasn't in her Sunday plans. Or any plans. But somehow, he got her talking. She wasn't sure why. Connie rarely talked about herself, to anyone. She'd endured enough talk a decade ago. Now she wanted obscurity. She wanted to stay in the shadows and avoid notoriety and gossip. And she certainly didn't want Jonah knowing anything about her past.

"What does that mean?" he asked quickly, frowning.

She shrugged, pushed off the memory that threatened to climb over her skin and moved a few things around on her desk. They *had* saved her, but it wasn't a story she wanted to tell. It was so long ago—rehashing the hurt and pain from those days was pointless. She'd made the commitment to move on with her life and not to look backward. "Nothing. I was just speaking metaphorically."

One dark brow came up. "Really?"

"I had some family stuff going on when I was younger. My parents had left town again and—"

"Again?" he queried, interrupting her.

"It's a long story," she replied. "Anyway, my grandfather had passed away, but I wanted to stay with my grandmother and I needed a job, so your dad gave me a chance here at the hotel. I'm grateful for that because it meant I could stay here and look after her."

"I thought you lived alone with your four dogs and your goldfish."

"I do," she replied, her uneasiness increasing, because she'd flown under the radar for so long it had been forever since she'd shared something personal about herself with anyone. And she'd never expected it to be with Jonah Rickard! And she was surprised that he remembered her comment about the dogs and goldfish. People didn't generally remember things about her—it was Connie who did the remembering. "Nan passed away three years ago."

His gaze darkened. "I'm sorry."

Connie shrugged one shoulder. "She was ill for a while, so her passing was a blessing."

"And your parents?"

"They don't live in Cedar River," she said as casually as she could, the usual ache she experienced when she thought of her parents quickly settling behind her rib cage. She'd stopped being angry with them a long time ago—now she felt only sadness and a heavy lingering regret that caught up with her on birthdays and around the holidays.

"I mean, why did they leave town?"

Connie shrugged. "For their work," she said and didn't elaborate.

"And you really like this town?" he asked. "I mean, that's why you stayed when your parents left?"

"I love Cedar River. It's my home."

"So you'll probably marry some local cowboy and settle down and have a bunch of kids?"

Connie looked at him. Damn, he was gorgeous. In dark jeans, a black shirt that stretched across his shoulders and a jacket she suspected had cost more than she made in a month, he was utterly and irrevocably the sexiest man she had ever met. And she wanted him. She wanted him so much that she'd almost had him...until the fear set in. Until her past rushed back to haunt her in ice-cold fashion. She wasn't sure why it had happened with Jonah—since he had somehow pushed her libido into overdrive from the first moment she'd clapped eyes on him. She'd hoped that her desire and the crazy chemistry between them would be enough to push past the barriers she'd erected around herself. Hoped...and failed. Not even her aching need for him had been enough. Instead, she'd panicked and run, denying her body the experience and release it craved.

"I'm not sure if I'll ever get married. But I believe in it," she said and shrugged. "You?"

"From what I've seen, marriage generally ends in divorce. So why bother?"

"Not all marriages end up that way," she offered. "Look at—"

"J.D. and Gwen?" he said, cutting her off. "Kieran and his ex-wife? Shall I go on?"

"They're bad examples," she said and rested her hips on the edge of her desk. "And J.D. and Gwen's marriage wasn't a complete disaster. They had thirty-five years together."

"Based on a lie," he said bitterly. "No, thanks."

Connie's heart rate increased. Talking about marriage got her thinking—because in her heart, she did want all that marriage offered: commitment, trust, the complete connection to another human being. But she often wondered if she'd ever have the courage for it. Or if she'd ever meet someone who would understand her fragile hold on trust and how achingly vulnerable she sometimes felt.

"Well, Kieran is happy now," she insisted. "And Liam and Kayla are desperately in love with one another. So obviously marriage *does* work…you just have to pick the right person."

"She's right," a deep voice said from across the room. "You do."

Liam.

He'd been her rock for a decade. Her friend and confidant as well as her boss, and she trusted him completely. Seeing him happy with Kayla and their baby son, Jack, made her feel all fuzzy inside. Liam deserved to be happy, and she was honored to call him her friend. He was the big brother she'd never had—the *family* she'd needed at the most desperate time in her life. If it weren't for Liam and J.D., Connie wasn't sure she would be as emotionally healthy as she was.

"If marriage is so great, why are you working on a Sunday?" Jonah asked cynically.

Liam sauntered across the room and grinned. "Because my pain-in-the-ass little brother is heading back to Portland tomorrow and we have some plans to go over."

Connie smiled and glanced toward Jonah. Even with his tightly clenched jaw and irritated expression, he was still the most handsome man she'd ever known. She looked for some level of affection between him and his brother but saw only disdain and impatience. And she felt sad for him, because the O'Sullivans had so much to offer and Jonah was too stubborn to see it.

She watched as the two men headed into Liam's office and heard them talking about the plans for the museum extension, and then she relaxed a little. Jonah was highly regarded in his field. An award-winning architect who'd designed buildings right along the West Coast, he was the youngest person to have ever made partner at Walters, Orsini & Rickard, a prestigious firm in Portland. J.D. had bragged about his many achievements countless times in the previous ten months, like any proud father would.

Twenty minutes later they were back in the main office. Liam passed her the folder and his electronic tablet and gave her a few instructions.

"I'll get Connie to email the details to you this week and you can start working up some plans," Liam said and nodded. "Okay?"

"Sure," Jonah replied. "No problem."

"Ah, Connie," Liam said and checked his watch. "If you can wait about half an hour, I'll go and speak with the sous chef and then drop you at home."

Before she had a chance to reply, Jonah spoke. "Don't you have a car?"

"It's in the shop," she supplied. "I can't pick it up until tomorrow. And Sean is using the hotel corporate car."

She noticed Jonah frown and shake his head slightly.

"I'll take her home," he said quietly to his brother and then met her gaze. "That way you won't have to hang around here."

Doormat.

The unsaid word hung in the air between them. Irritation snaked up her spine and she smiled sweetly. "I wouldn't want to impose."

"You won't be," he said and pulled keys from his pocket. "Let's go."

Connie ignored Liam's curious expression and quickly gathered her tote and laptop, aware that he was watching her movements and was probably wondering what was going on between them. To his credit, Liam didn't say anything, but she suspected she'd be on the receiving end of a few questions the following day.

Five minutes later she was being driven from the parking area in Jonah's stylish Lexus.

"Nice car," she remarked, stroking the soft leather seat. "Very…understated."

"What did you expect?" he asked, his mouth curved into a half smile.

"Oh, I don't know…maybe a red Corvette."

"Flashy isn't my thing," he remarked and pulled out onto Main Street. "I like things that are low-maintenance."

Connie looked straight ahead. "Girls, too?"

"Girls, too," he replied. "I guess that counts you out."

"I'm not high-maintenance," Connie stated, ignoring the heat suffusing her cheeks.

He chuckled. "Oh, you're about as high as it gets."

"Because I wouldn't have sex with you?" she demanded. "That's just your macho conditioning talking."

He laughed and turned the car off Main Street, heading toward the bridge and over the river. "I have been turned down before, you know. Maybe not in such dramatic fashion. Or at such a…" His words trailed off for a moment. "Let's call it a pivotal moment."

Because your hand was up my skirt.

Like a camera speeding in reverse, Connie was suddenly back in his hotel room, feeling every touch, every kiss, every breath. And remembering how much she'd wanted him, how perfect his broad shoulders felt beneath her hands, how insanely erotic his kisses were. And then she remembered the rest—the fear clawing up her back, the feeling of suffocation, the sense that she was out of control…and that her body was someone else's and not her own to command.

"I shouldn't have gone to your room," she said quietly. "You were right to be annoyed."

"No, Connie," he said, his voice just as quiet. "I wasn't. It was your right to say no."

"Thank you."

"I am curious, though," he said softly. "Did I do something to offend you? Was I too—"

"No," she said quickly, eager to end the conversation. "It wasn't you. It was me. I think I just panicked and—"

"You have nothing to fear from me, Connie," he said, cutting her off. "Then or now."

Heat burned her eyes. Because she knew that whatever else he was, Jonah Rickard was trustworthy and honorable. "I know that." She looked around and blinked, forcing the heat away and realized they were nowhere near her street. "Um…where are we going?"

"If you don't mind, I thought we could make a short detour," he said casually and turned into a wide, leafy street.

"A detour?" she echoed, panic skirting along the edges of her spine for a moment. She dismissed the idea quickly. Jonah was not a threat. "To where?"

He pulled up outside a low-set, brick home with shuttered windows and a wide porch. "My mother's."

Connie had met Kathleen Rickard several times. Not quite fifty, she was a petite, attractive woman with pale hair and green eyes and was quite lovely. She hooked a thumb sideways. "This is your mom's house?"

He nodded. "We can leave if you prefer."

She saw the curtains move. "I think she knows we're here."

"So, we'll go inside?"

Connie nodded warily. "I guess so."

A minute later they were on the porch and the front door opened. Kathleen greeted her son with a warm embrace that was filled with love and devotion, and Connie experienced a sharp pang of envy. It wasn't that her parents hadn't loved her—she was sure they had, and still did, in their own way. But they were never very good at being *parents*. Kathleen, however, looked as though she would move heaven and earth to protect her only son. And in a way, she had. She'd left Cedar River when she'd gotten pregnant and made a new life for herself and her baby.

"Sweetie," Kathleen said and touched Jonah's face. "It's so good to see you."

"Mom," he said with a groan and shook his head. "Don't call me sweetie, okay?"

Kathleen laughed. "I'll try not to. And Connie, it's lovely to see you again. Jonah didn't tell me he was bringing a…friend with him today."

Heat crawled up her neck. "I'm just tagging along," she explained. "I was working for a few hours today and my car is in the shop, so I needed a lift home from the hotel. I hope it's okay that I'm here?"

"Of course," Kathleen said, ushering them inside and down the hallway. "I'm delighted."

The house was modest but tastefully decorated, and when they reached the living area, Connie noticed that one corner was filled with canvases and artist's tools, including an assortment of easels and several small tables crammed with paints and charcoals.

"You're an artist?" she asked.

Kathleen shrugged lightly. "I dabble. Though I'm not really very good. It's more of a hobby than anything else."

Connie noticed one of the largest easels was covered in a paint-splattered sheet. "Is that a secret project?"

Kathleen grinned. "More of a practice piece. I'm branching out into portraits. You know, you have lovely bone structure," she commented and nodded and looked at her son. "She'd make a great model. Don't you think, sweetie?"

"Mom," Jonah chastised. "Enough with the sweetie thing."

Connie wasn't sure if he was genuinely embarrassed, but Kathleen took it in stride. They were clearly very close and a tight unit.

"Okay, I promise," his mother said and shrugged. "Now, go and be useful and bring me some firewood," she said and pointed to the empty crate near the hearth. "It's going to get cold this week, and I'd like to be ready for the turn in the weather. It's out by the back door."

He lingered for a moment before leaving the room, his loose-limbed stride becoming so familiar to Connie that she suspected she could pick him out in a crowd at a hundred yards.

"So," Kathleen said once he was out of sight. "Tell me, Connie…how long have you been dating my son?"

By the time he had the second hunk of firewood in his arms, Jonah figured that bringing Connie to his mother's home was up there with some of the stupidest things he'd ever done. Because he knew from the look in his mom's eyes that she was imagining all kinds of things—most of them focused on Connie being the first girl he'd brought home in nearly five years. Of course, like any mother, she had the matchmaking bug. And she wanted grandchildren…she'd made that clear on countless occasions. And yeah, maybe one day he'd find someone and raise a family. *Maybe.* One thing was for sure—he'd do a damned better job being a father than J.D. ever had.

By the time he returned to the living room, Connie was alone.

"Did you get the third degree?" he asked and dumped the firewood.

"Yes," she replied. "It took several minutes of fast talking to convince her that I am not your girlfriend."

He grinned. "That's better than I expected. But in her defense, I don't make a habit of bringing girls home to meet my mother."

Something flashed in her eyes—something that had everything to do with the attraction that pulsed undeniably between them.

"So, why did you bring me?" she asked, brows up.

Jonah managed a shrug. "I don't really know."

She smiled. "I figured you'd be the kind of man who knows exactly what he's doing at every moment. Or at least, that's what you want people to think."

Jonah's mouth curled at the edges. "That sounds like more criticism."

"It's an observation," she said, still smiling. "I see you, Jonah. I see what's underneath your arrogance and resentment. You're actually a lot nicer than you make out."

Jonah grimaced. "Nah… I'm not."

She chuckled. "It's not a flaw, you know. Or a weakness."

"It just feels like one, right?" he offered and shrugged a little. "Anyway, I'm sorry if my mom gave you the third degree."

"She thinks you're afraid of commitment."

"Wary," he corrected. "There's a difference. I guess she's in the kitchen making tea?"

She nodded. "She loves you a lot."

"I know," he said. "It's mutual."

"You're lucky. No everyone gets that."

There was pain in her voice, and it gave him an odd ache inside. "Didn't you?"

"Not in the way you did," she replied. "My parents were…*are*…hard to get close to. They're career focused. Archaeologists," she explained when he frowned. "The truth is, I spent most of my early childhood living on one excavation site after another, but when I was eight they sent me back here to live permanently with my grandparents. They parented me the best they could when they came back in between trips, but since they'd never planned on having kids, most of the time they were a train wreck. At the moment they're in South America somewhere, but I don't hear from them very often. I'm very grateful that I had my grandparents." She sighed, then took a breath, and when she met his gaze, her eyes were brighter than usual. "I don't know why I told you that."

"I'm not judging. Just listening."

"I know," she said and dropped onto the sofa. "You're good at it. It's very annoying."

Jonah laughed softly. "Some people think it's charming."

"Some women, you mean?" she suggested. "You've probably had women standing in line for you since you hit puberty."

"Not quite," he admitted. "I was something of a geek in high school. And puny. And I had braces."

"That paints quite a picture. I imagined you were the quarterback with cheerleaders hanging off your every word."

"No. A computer geek. I didn't really discover girls until college."

"Did you make up for lost time?"

Jonah's blood quickened. "I did my best. What about you? Were you the most popular girl in high school?"

She shook her head. "Not by a long mile. Book nerd."

"No high school boyfriend to take you to prom?"

"I didn't go to prom. I left high school at end of my sophomore year."

Surprised, he asked the obvious question. "You didn't graduate?"

"I was homeschooled by my grandmother. She used to be a teacher. I started working at the hotel before graduation and J.D. offered me a full-time job when I got my diploma, but he insisted I get a college degree no matter what. So I achieved my BA through online courses."

"Why didn't you go to school and college the usual way?" he asked quietly.

She shrugged casually. Too casually, he thought. But she replied. "I just didn't fit in at school. But I was determined to get an education."

Admiration settled behind his ribs. It was a harder road than he'd had, that was for sure. Jonah had spent his elementary years at private school and high school years at the best educational facility Portland had to offer. J.D. hadn't neglected his financial support on his secret family. It was everywhere else that he'd failed in the parenting department.

His mother returned a few moments later, carrying a tray and looking delighted, and he knew he was in for a load of questions the next time he visited alone. As he looked around the room, he realized how much change had occurred in the house since she'd moved in a few months earlier. There were pictures on the walls now, and a large framed landscape above the fireplace. And a few plants were scattered around the room in heavy ceramic pots.

"You've been decorating," he remarked, realizing there was a large oak dresser against one wall. "I would have come and moved things if you needed help with furniture."

He noticed his mother's gaze darted downward. "Oh, yes, I had a friend give me a hand. It was just a few things and I didn't want to disturb you."

"Which friend?" he asked.

His mother smiled and waved a hand. "No one you know. So, Connie…what are your plans for Thanksgiving this year?"

"The same as last year," she replied. "I volunteer at the veterans' home near the community hospital when I can, and over the holidays I lend a hand serving the turkey and baked ham. Then I head to a friend's place and have drinks with her. Sometimes I work—it depends on how busy things are at the hotel. The O'Sullivans always invite me to spend the day with them, but I don't like to impose."

She was jabbering…nervously. Almost as though she was embarrassed by her lack of family to spend the holidays with. Jonah experienced an acute sense of sympathy and respect. And although he was sure she rarely allowed anyone to see it, there was a kind of vulnerability about Connie that pushed his sense of honor and instinctively made him want to protect her…though he had no idea what from. Especially since she seemed capable and strong and very able to look after herself.

But the macho conditioning she'd accused him of having suddenly kicked in and he spoke before he had the chance to realize what he was saying. "You'd be welcome to join us."

She stared at him, wide-eyed. "Oh…well… I…"

"Yes," his mother chimed in. "That's a lovely idea. The more the merrier. Sometimes it is awfully quiet when it's just the two of us. And if Jonah is in one of his *moods*… well…"

"Moods?" he echoed. "What moods?"

The two women looked straight-faced for a moment and then burst out laughing.

"Sweetie," his mother said and ignored his scowl, "you know how you get all worked up about things. He gets that from my side of the family," she said and winked toward Connie. "My brother, Derek, gets like that…quiet and closed off."

"Would you stop talking about me as though I'm not in the room?" he requested, not as outraged as he probably should have been, because Connie's smile sparked something deep inside him. Something that brought on an uncomfortable urge to kiss her. Pushing the feeling aside, he pretended to glare at his mother, reminding her, "And don't call me sweetie."

"Yes, dear," she said and poured the tea. "It's because he's a Virgo."

Jonah groaned. "Please, Mom, not the astrology thing."

"Oh, please go on," Connie said and took the cup his mother offered, her gray eyes sparkling delightfully. "This I'd like to hear."

Jonah stood back, suddenly poleaxed, as he realized an astounding fact. Despite the way they sparred and their complicated history, he liked Connie. And it wasn't merely a byproduct of the insane sexual desire he felt for her. He genuinely *liked* her. He wanted to get to know her better. He wanted to see her smile and hear her laugh and pick up the scent of her perfume on his clothes after they'd spent time together.

And he was, he also realized, going to pursue her.

Whatever it took, he was going to get her into his bed and see if he could purge the feelings that were banging around in his mind and body. Because there was no walking away from Connie Bedford. She'd gotten under his skin and the only way to get her out was to dive in, headfirst.

He'd have her in his arms—and in his bed—by Thanksgiving.

He was sure of it.

Connie enjoyed chatting with Kathleen Rickard. The other woman entertained her with stories about her life in Portland and her work as kindergarten teacher—and about Jonah as a child, which clearly embarrassed him a little. She relaxed and sat back into the couch, conscious that Jonah was sitting across the room on a damask love seat, watching her over the rim of his mug. He seemed content to keep quiet and allow Kathleen to monopolize the conversation. But she felt the intensity of his stare as though he was branding her skin with his fingertips. His blue eyes remained solely fixed on her for the following half hour, and her awareness of him was on red alert.

It was nearly twelve when he suggested they leave, and she agreed without complaint. Kathleen made her promise to think about Thanksgiving, and Connie assured her she'd be in touch.

Once they were in the car and back on the road, Connie noticed that he was still silent. "Is everything okay?" she asked.

"Of course," he replied and then asked for her address again.

"Your mother is so lovely. I had a nice time."

"I'm glad."

"Why didn't she ever get married?" she asked quietly.

His fingers tightened on the steering wheel. "Because she could never completely finish things with J.D."

Connie couldn't miss the condemnation in his voice, and her heart lurched. "I don't understand."

"He kept coming around…kept giving her hope."

"But their romantic relationship had ended, right?" she probed. "When she left Cedar River, didn't she end things between them?"

"Yeah," he replied and took a right turn. "But he still made himself a fixture in her life."

"In your life," she corrected. "He visited Portland to see *you*, correct?"

He shrugged aggressively. "So he says. And thankfully Mom has always kept him at arm's length. But his constant presence made it impossible for *her* to move on with her life, so she didn't."

"Did you want her to?"

"I wanted her to be happy," he replied. "I still do. I'm just not sure how she can do it here with so many memories."

"What do you mean? She's been gone for over thirty years, hasn't she?"

He shrugged again. "People talk…gossip is inevitable. She had an affair with a married man, a very wealthy man from the most prominent family in town. And as much as I hate the idea of anyone thinking badly of her, mud sticks. But she doesn't seem to care. She says she wants to spend some time with her brother and mother. And I have to support her because it's her decision."

"She seems happy," Connie suggested. "I mean, from an outsider's point of view."

"Are you an expert on happiness?"

"I like to think I live an authentic life," she said, glancing sideways and noticing how the pulse in his jaw throbbed. "Do you?"

"Mostly. I try to always tell the truth, even when it's hard."

"Except to your father."

Once the words were out, she couldn't take them back, particularly since they sounded like an accusation.

"I've always been honest with J.D., so he knows exactly how I feel about him."

Connie stared at the pulse in his cheek some more, counting as the beats increased. "Anger is a wasted emotion. So if that's what you feel toward him, maybe it's time you let it go. He made mistakes, but who hasn't? None of us can change the past."

I know that better than anyone.

"And if I said I was indifferent?"

"I wouldn't believe you," she replied quietly. "You're too…intense for indifference."

He laughed softly. "You know, it came out sounding like a compliment, but I'm sure it's not meant to be."

She grinned. "Maybe we bring out the worst in one another."

"Or the best," he said and turned onto her street. "Depending on your perspective."

Before she had a chance to respond, he pulled up outside her house. A familiar warmth spread through her blood at the sight of the large cottage, with its wraparound porch and stained glass windows. The place had belonged to her grandparents, and now it was hers. She did her best to maintain her grandmother's once picture-perfect garden, but mostly settled for easy-to-manage shrubs, and recently she'd added pots of chrysanthemums in vivid fall colors on the porch. Still, the old oak tree behind the white picket fence made the place look like it belonged on a postcard.

"Cute," he said. "Exactly how I would have pictured

it. I bet you have one of those kitchens with pots hanging above the stove. I'll even bet that you make your own jelly."

He was right on both accounts. Connie had been making her grandmother's famous plum jam since she was a little girl. "Well, nothing wrong with being a little predictable."

"No," he said, his blue eyes deepening, and suddenly the space between them became intensely intimate. "Nothing wrong with that at all."

She watched as his gaze dropped to her mouth and her lips instantly tingled. *He wants to kiss me.* Her belly dipped and she let out a shallow sigh. They could argue about anything and everything, they could disagree about the most basic issues, but still the attraction between them lingered, finding a life force of its own whenever it had the opportunity.

"I should…I should go. Thank you for the ride."

Connie heard a bark, and then another. Her dogs were always on point and came rushing around from the backyard. Ruffalo, a wolfhound mix and the largest of the group, jumped up at the gate and let out a long howl.

"You seem to have plenty of protection back there." Jonah gazed past her at the leaping dogs.

She nodded. "They look after me. Keep me safe." She placed her fingers on the door handle and went to open the door, but he spoke again.

"Connie?"

She sucked in a breath. "Yes."

"Have dinner with me on Friday?"

Dinner? "What? Why?"

He reached out and grasped her chin gently, his thumb scraping across her bottom lip in a way that was so sexy she could barely breathe. His gaze was dark and intense, his chest moving with every breath he took.

"Because I would like to go on a date with you."

"To what end?"

He didn't flinch. "To get to know you better."

"And?"

He sighed. "And at the end of our date I would like to kiss you good-night." His thumb moved over her mouth again, dipping slightly inside.

"And then?" she managed, wondering from where she harnessed the nerve.

He shrugged one magnificent shoulder. "And then at some point, when you're ready, I'd very much like to make love to you."

It was the most erotic thing anyone had ever said to her. And the fact that it was Jonah saying the words to her made the moment even more earth-shatteringly intense. She stared at his handsome face, looking for some sign that he couldn't possibly mean it, that he was playing some kind of cruel joke, and found only hot, passionate honesty.

"I'll be back in Cedar River on Friday," he said and dropped his hand. "I'll pick you up at seven. Wear shoes that you can dance in. Okay?"

She found herself nodding vaguely, grabbed her tote and quickly got out of the car, noticing that he didn't drive off until she was safely on the porch, with the dogs jumping and yapping around her.

Connie felt as though she'd suddenly stepped into her own private fairy tale.

But she couldn't possibly do it. She'd promised herself that she would put an end to any foolish fantasizing about Jonah. Because he'd made it clear what he wanted. The endgame was sex. She'd turned him down ten months ago, bruised his ego, and now he wanted to even the score. Which meant there was no way in hell she was going on a date with him.

But through the haze of sensibleness and rational reasoning, Connie was feeling something else as well. Anticipation. Because it didn't matter how much time she spent on denials or self-reflection, the outcome was always the same. For some unfathomable reason, despite knowing that he was intolerant and judgmental and refused to accept his place within the O'Sullivan family, Connie was inexplicably drawn toward Jonah. Mostly, her life was about the hotel, her friends and her dogs. Romance took a back seat. Sure, she went on the occasional date, but that was usually as far as it went. But Jonah was different. Jonah was exciting. He made her feel more alive than she had felt before. And despite her good sense telling her that she should refuse his dinner invitation, Connie was tempted. It was just dinner. Maybe a light flirtation. A kiss or two. She could handle that. All she had to do was work out a way to deal with her budding feelings.

Without getting her heart well and truly broken.

Chapter Four

Jonah had one motive for returning to Cedar River the following Friday.

Connie.

He ditched work early Friday and took a four-and-a-half-hour flight, followed by a forty-minute cab ride from Rapid City to the small town, which meant it was nearly six when he pulled up outside the old Victorian. He showered, changed, checked his emails and then left to pick up Connie.

He arrived at her house at five to seven, and as he walked to her front door, he realized he was uncharacteristically nervous. He rapped twice and waited, hearing the scramble of countless paws over floorboards and a cacophony of loud barking before the door swung back. Her dogs were at her side, standing behind the screen as she shushed them.

"Sorry about that," she said. "They go a little nuts when they hear anyone at the door."

Jonah looked down and the smallest of the trio, a mean-looking black-and-white terrier, growled low in its throat. He managed a smile. "I'm glad you're well protected." He glanced up and down, taking in her knee-length blue dress and heeled boots, and his gut clenched. "You look pretty."

"Dancing shoes," she said and pointed to her feet as she opened the storm door. "Although we've already established that I can't dance."

Jonah grinned. "That's the point. You ready to go?"

She nodded, slipped on her coat, pulled a bag over her shoulder and locked the screen, making reassuring noises to the dogs as she closed the door. "All set."

Jonah automatically pressed a supportive hand to the small of her back as they headed down the steps, and she jerked slightly. "Sorry," he said and dropped his hand.

She shrugged. "It's fine. I just haven't been on a date in while."

"Me, either," he admitted, opening the gate so they could step onto the sidewalk.

"So where are we going?" she asked once they were buckled up in his Lexus. "I'm guessing O'Sullivans?"

"No," he replied and turned the ignition. "I promised you dancing, remember?"

She chuckled. "You'll be sorry."

Jonah laughed and realized his stomach was no longer churning. She had a way of doing that…a way of steadying his demeanor. As they drove through town, she chatted about the hotel and his mother and asked him about his week. Jonah replied in monosyllables, content to hear her speak, finding her voice relaxed him. He'd foolishly been anxious all week, thinking about seeing her again. A part of him had expected her to call and cancel—or, worse, to shut the door in his face when he'd arrived on her doorstep.

"I should have brought you flowers," he said, almost talking to himself.

"Oh…so this is a *real* date?"

"Of course," he said, looking straight ahead. "Were you expecting something else?"

He almost heard her shrug. "I don't have any expectations. Just know that, despite how my previous behavior might suggest something to the contrary," she said and took a shallow breath, "I'm not…*easy*."

"I know that. And for the record," he said as he took the highway route and began the twenty-six-mile drive to their destination, "if I was only interested in getting laid I could have stayed in Portland, gone out with friends to a nightclub and picked up someone who *was*."

She made a sound—like a disapproving huff mixed with a surprised gasp—and then spoke. "Do you think you're that irresistible?"

Jonah's mouth twisted. "Not at all. But these days, casual sex isn't hard to find, if that's all you're after."

"Which makes it sound as though it's something you do regularly," she remarked tightly.

"No," he replied quickly. "I don't."

She clutched her bag in her lap. "I'm glad to hear it. But I'm still not going to sleep with you tonight."

"Okay," he said and heard her relax.

"And you're fine with that?" she asked, glancing at him for a moment. "I mean…isn't that why you asked me out and—"

"I'm fine with that," he cut her off quietly. "It's your decision."

She sighed. "Okay…thank you."

"You sound like you expected a different answer."

"I'm not sure what I expect when it comes to you."

Jonah laughed softly. "I think that's a compliment… right?"

"I'm not sure," she said. "You confuse me. I mean, most of the time you're unbearable. But then, other times, you're actually quite reasonable."

"Reasonable?"

"Likable," she said quietly. "I don't know…sort of… sweet."

"Sweet?"

She chuckled. "Okay, maybe that's a stretch. But you can't really be as awful as everyone thinks, right? I mean, you're very nice to your mom."

"She's my mother," he said mildly. "Of course I'm nice to her."

"Not everyone gets along with their parents, believe me."

He heard the pain in her voice, and it made his insides crunch up. "Are your folks that bad?"

"No," she replied. "But they were never interested in being parents. They were always focused on their careers, and I was a distraction they didn't want or need."

"You must hate them."

"Not at all," she said, twisting the handle of her tote. "I don't believe in hate."

"Hate's an emotion. Human beings feel emotions. You can't deny that hate exists."

"I'm not," she said quickly. "Put it this way—I don't allow hate into my life. Or rage. Or anger. Or despair. It's feels like a waste of emotional energy."

Jonah was intrigued by her words. "So, you've never been angry? Never hated anyone?"

"I didn't say that," she replied. "Sure, when I was younger, sometimes I did experience those things. But now I *choose* to live a different sort of life."

"That's a very controlled view of things."

"That's me," she said quietly. "Always in control. Unlike you, someone at the mercy of their emotions."

Jonah laughed out loud. "Seriously? That's what you think? What happened to my reputation as a cold, unfeeling—"

"That's your disguise," she said, cutting him off. "I've seen you with the two people you care about most—your mom and dad."

Jonah almost brought the car to a screeching halt on the shoulder. He gripped the steering wheel and concentrated on the road ahead. "I don't care about J.D."

"Sure you do," she answered flippantly. "Love and hate—sometimes they're not so different."

"Psychoanalysis 101. I didn't realize you sidelined as a shrink."

"I went to…" Her words trailed off and she took a breath. "I know a little about it."

"That's reassuring."

She laughed softly. "You really are impossible sometimes. I can't imagine how much energy it takes to be so obnoxious. You know, if you were more pleasant, you'd make more friends."

"I have enough friends," he said and eased into the right lane, preparing to exit the highway.

"Your mom told me you've never had a serious relationship."

"Did she?" he shot back. "Clearly she talks too much. We're here," he said as he took the exit and headed in the parking area of their destination.

"The honky-tonk place?" she inquired, leaning forward in her seat as he parked the car, staring at the huge restaurant, which had been built to resemble an old saloon, with a wraparound porch and shuttered windows.

"I've heard about it. The girls have been saying we should—"

"The girls?" he asked, as he unclipped his seat belt.

"Nicola and Annie, a friend of mine. The restaurant is giving O'Sullivans a run for its money."

He shrugged. "I don't really know what goes on at the hotel. Although I'm sure Liam's head is spinning at the idea of some competition…even if it is nearly thirty miles away."

He was out of the car in a few seconds and came around to the passenger side just as she was stepping out onto the gravel. Her perfume swirled around them, mixing with the cool night air like a seductive tonic. She looked so beautiful in her dress and woolen coat, and Jonah resisted the urge to haul her into his arms and kiss her. The truth was, he'd thought about little else for the past week. The taste of her lips was a sweet memory and he couldn't shake the idea. He wanted her. In his arms. In his bed.

"You look really pretty. I'm not sure if I said that already."

She glanced up and met his gaze as he closed the door and locked the car. "Um…you did. But I like hearing it."

Heat clawed at his skin. Without even trying, Connie could make him feel about sixteen.

"Let's go."

The place was busy, filled with cowboys, cowgirls and a seven-piece band belting out country tunes. Not Jonah's taste at all, since he was more of a classic rock fan, but he noticed that Connie was tapping her toe as they waited to be seated and figured he'd picked right, hoping that she liked country music.

"Not too much?" he asked as a waitress decked out in

red gingham outfit walked past carrying a tray loaded with barbecued ribs and hot sauce.

She smiled. "Nope. And I'm hungry."

He returned the smile, enjoying that she was clearly in a good mood, and relaxed a little more. He was happy that she wasn't tense or looking like she wanted to be somewhere else.

"I wasn't sure you'd come tonight," he remarked as they were shown to their table.

She slipped off her coat and draped it over the back of the chair and then sat. "I didn't really have a choice, did I?"

"You always have a choice with me," he replied.

She met his gaze straight on. "That means a lot."

He wasn't sure why it would. Maybe she was just fiercely independent and liked to do things in her own time and way. Still, there was something about Connie that fueled his protective mode. It wasn't weakness... more like a vulnerability simmering below the surface. A vulnerability she didn't want anyone to see. But Jonah saw it and felt it. And somehow, knowing she was allowing him into that part of herself scared him to death.

Connie knew she was getting in way over her head. But damn... Jonah looked so handsome and sexy in his dark suit and white shirt and she was, she'd discovered, foolishly susceptible to his charms. During the past week she'd thought of every reason why she shouldn't go out with him, and in the sensible part of her brain, every reason made perfect sense. Even Liam had warned her off in his own way, making some off-the-cuff comment about Jonah being the most disagreeable human on the planet. But she didn't really agree with him. Sure, she and Jonah were different. He could be an arrogant jerk sometimes. And she knew it wouldn't—couldn't—really go anywhere. The truth was, she'd labored on the idea for a week, avoiding Liam's comments about his brother, confiding only in Annie, leaving out the part about that night in his hotel room all those months ago. By Friday around lunchtime she'd talked herself out of going.

But still, once she got home that afternoon, she'd found herself sorting through her wardrobe and looking for something to wear. Including dancing shoes.

Idiot.

Going on a date with Jonah Rickard was her dumbest move yet. All he'd had to do was turn up on time and tell her how nice she looked and she was done for. And she liked the fact that he hadn't settled for a predictably intimate dinner at O'Sullivan's for their first official date. The honky-tonk, a crowded and rowdy place filled with cowboys, marinated ribs, checkered shirts and country music, was exactly the opposite of what she had expected, or what she was used to. Usually she was taken to quiet, respectable establishments because her dates always assumed that suited her personality. However, the truth was, she liked country music, horses, cowboy boots, battered fries and thick steaks covered in gravy. Perhaps because it was the complete opposite of how she appeared during her usual working day—with her corporate suit, tightly upswept hairstyle and sensible patent heels.

She liked that he knew her well enough to figure she was more than simply a woman in a suit.

"Thank you for bringing me here," she said once their drink order had been taken. "It was an unexpected surprise."

His expression softened. "My pleasure."

"You even reserved a table."

"Of course," he replied. "Have your past dates been so disastrous?"

Connie laughed softly. "Not all of them. Although there was this one guy last year who bailed halfway through because he got a text from his ex."

Jonah's brows shot upward. "You're not serious."

"Yep. Left before dessert. At least he paid the check on the way out."

"Chivalry is alive and well, then," he said wryly and glanced at the menu. "Although he sounds like a real jerk." Jonah met her gaze. "He'd have to be to leave you alone in a restaurant."

Connie's insides clenched. "So, I was right, you *are* sweet."

His mouth curled at the edges. "You know, I don't think I've ever been called that before."

"Except by your mom," she remarked and sipped her wine spritzer and grinned. "She calls you sweetie."

"You remember that?"

Connie nodded. "She loves you a lot. It's nice. And makes me a little envious."

The waitress returned and took their meal order, and once the other woman was gone, Jonah spoke again. "I'm sure your parents care about you."

She shrugged, blinking back the heat suddenly burning behind her eyes. "I suppose they do, in their own way."

"How long since you've seen them?"

"Three years," she replied quietly.

"Since your grandmother's funeral?" he suggested.

Connie stared at him, realizing it was the first time anyone had really noticed that fact. Not that she talked about her parents to anyone in any great depth—not even her closest friend, Annie. But she was startled that he'd picked up on the correlation between her absent parents and the loss of her much-loved grandmother.

She nodded. "They prefer to be in a tent on the edge of

some excavation site in a foreign country than in Cedar River. Once Nan passed away, I guess they stopped thinking they had any reason to return."

"Except you?" he queried and then spoke again before she could respond. "Do you have any other family?"

She shrugged again. "My mother wasn't from here, so her attachment isn't very strong. Her parents were from Wyoming and died years ago. She has a brother in Cheyenne, so I have a few cousins who live around there, although a Christmas card is about as connected as we are to each other. And my dad is an only child like me. I have a great-aunt who was a teacher at some private school in Boise. She never married or had kids. So, there you have it…my meager family tree. Do you feel sorry for me now?"

"Not especially," he replied. "I don't think pity is quite your style."

He was so right she was stunned. "It's not. I'm far too independent. Sure, I would have liked to have a sibling or two…but I'm not one to pine after what I don't have."

"Siblings are overrated," he said and sipped the imported beer he'd ordered.

"Easy for you to say," she shot back. "You have a bunch of brothers."

"Half brothers," he corrected.

Connie's spine straightened. "It's really infuriating the way you do that."

He shrugged lightly. "I'm not going to pretend they mean more to me than they do."

"I don't think you should," she replied. "But you could give them a chance. And yes," she said before he could speak. "I know you've made the occasional effort, like helping Kieran and Nicola design that pond in her backyard. And I know you went to Gwen's birthday party even though every instinct you possess probably screamed for you to stay away, but since you admire Gwen, you went anyway."

He shrugged lightly. "It was the polite thing to do."

She nodded. "Yes, you're right. So I know you *have* tried...or maybe it's more about taking the path of least resistance. Then again, I wouldn't peg you as someone who would choose the easy road."

He chuckled. "You have me."

Connie's insides lurched. Because his words were suggestive and provocative, and for a few crazy seconds she *wished* they were true. But she was terrified of where that might lead. Jonah was not the kind of man a woman could dismiss and forget. Jonah was the kind of man who broke hearts...even if he didn't mean to.

She shifted the subject, asking him about his work, and he answered her questions, adding in a few anecdotes about his life in Oregon. The more he spoke, the deeper she was drawn in, resting her chin on the back of her hand, listening intently, eager to catch every word. There was nothing moody or arrogant about him in that moment. He was pleasant and friendly and funny and *nice*. It occurred to Connie that despite how much he tried to hide it, she was seeing who he really was. A side of himself he didn't often show in Cedar River.

Once their meals arrived, they stopped talking for a while, except for Jonah's comment about her pile of marinated ribs. She glanced at the grilled fish he'd ordered and wrinkled up her nose.

"City boy," she said and grinned, picking up a sticky rib.

He laughed. "Watch your fingers."

"I'm an expert at barbecued ribs," she announced. "And pizza. What about you?"

"Chopsticks."

"Show-off," she said and then ate.

By the time they were done with their meal, close to an hour had passed. Connie learned that Jonah rarely ate red meat, that he was allergic to pineapple and loved ice cream. He admitted to being a lousy cook and told her about the cat that somehow managed to find a way into the apartment when he stayed there.

"Sounds like you've made another friend in Cedar River," she said when the waitress took their plates away. "The cat obviously likes you."

"*Another* friend?"

She shrugged. "Well, I haven't quite put you into the friends category yet. But you're growing on me."

"Like a fungus?" he suggested, a smile crinkling his mouth.

"You heard about that?" she asked, remembering how she'd made that comparison about him to his brother and Nicola a few weeks earlier.

"I heard," he said and smiled. "Kieran thought it was hilarious."

Heat burned her cheeks. "Sorry."

He smiled again. "I can take a little criticism, particularly when I've behaved badly enough to deserve it."

Compassion surged through her veins. "It must have been hard coming to this town and confronting everyone."

"It was," he replied. "Sometimes it still is. But that first time I wasn't about to let my mom turn up and face it alone. She wanted her brother and J.D. to make peace, and for the sake of Liam and Kayla's marriage, believed the only way she could do that was to come home and deal with it all in person."

Connie rested her elbows on the table. "Do you hate them as much as you make out?"

"Yes."

She sucked in a breath. "Oh, well, I—"

"And no," he added and shrugged. "Most of the time I try not to think about it. But they don't let me off the hook so easily. Particularly Liam and Kieran."

"You're their brother, so it's natural that they want to have some sort of relationship with you."

He sat back in his seat. "It should be easy, right? But it's not."

"Because you're stubborn?"

"You *could* call me that, I suppose."

There was a sudden noise, like glass breaking, and then raised voices, and Connie's instincts surged into overdrive, making her feel things she didn't want to feel. Long-buried feelings that she tried to keep at bay. Like fear. At one end of the bar, she spotted a group of rowdy cowboys who were causing a scene with a couple of the waitresses. The bartender had moved around the counter; a tall, well-built man she suspected was the restaurant manager quickly harnessed the group and the rowdy men quieted down immediately.

"Are you okay?" Jonah asked and briefly touched her arm.

Connie's skin tingled and she looked at his fingers as he pulled his hand away. She crossed her arms and shivered. "I'm not good with sudden noises. Or rowdy people. But I'm fine now."

He didn't look convinced. "I wouldn't let anything happen to you."

Connie's throat tightened immediately. *Where were you ten years ago?* She pushed the thought aside, ignoring the old and yet still familiar pain winding up her spine. Without really knowing why, she felt safe with Jonah.

"I know you wouldn't."

His expression lightened. "Would you like to dance?"

Connie glanced at the crowded dance floor. "You'll be sorry."

He chuckled and stood, holding out his hand. "I'll risk it. Let's go."

She left her coat on the back of the chair, looping her small bag over her shoulder as she took his hand and rose to her feet. His fingers curled around hers and he led the way as they wove through the dancers and found a spot in the center. The band was playing a midtempo love song, and several couples were swaying around them. He halted, placed one hand on her hip and drew her closer.

"So, what should I do?" she asked, looking up at him, her mouth barely reaching his chin.

He really was remarkably handsome, and his blue eyes glittered brilliantly. "Just hold on to me."

She nodded and placed one hand on his shoulder, while the other stayed entwined with his hand. Palm to palm, hip to hip, with enough distance between them to appear respectable, Connie was achingly aware of the intimacy being so close to him evoked. Her fingers burned against his shoulder, even through layers of clothing, and the scent of the cologne he wore was unbelievably arousing. She hadn't been this close to anyone since… since that crazy night in his hotel room. And she liked the feelings he evoked within her.

Even if she was scared to death of acting on them.

"You're tense," he said and gently drew her closer. "Relax."

"I warned you that I couldn't dance."

He held her gaze. "You're not so bad."

Connie swayed against him, experiencing an awareness that was so acute, her entire body was suddenly on fire. She'd never had that kind of reaction to a man before. She wanted him. But the very idea was at odds with everything she believed him to be. At least, what she *had* believed.

Now, Connie wasn't so sure. They were on a date. He was polite and charming and perfectly respectable. He wasn't at all the way everyone else believed him to be. And if she dared allow herself to really think about it, Connie hadn't ever truly believed he was like that. Not since that night in the bar at O'Sullivans when they'd talked with a kind of raw earnestness that had reached her deep down. That's why she'd gone to his room, why she'd kissed him like there was no tomorrow.

"You're not so bad, either," she said and looked up, meeting his gaze, feeling the heat emanating from him, and then drowning in his blue eyes. "I don't know what to make of this."

"This?"

"You and me," she replied, noticing that his grip tightened just a fraction. "It seems kind of out of left field. I'm not sure everyone would understand."

"Everyone? You mean the O'Sullivans?" His brows came up. "J.D. has already warned me to stay away from you."

"He's just looking out for me."

"I accused him of being infatuated with you," he admitted, and despite her instant annoyance toward him for being so ridiculous, she also admired his honesty. "But that's not it. This codependence thing you've got going with J.D. and Liam and even Gwen…it's about something else. Maybe it's because of Liz's death. I imagine losing a sister, a daughter, was devastating for the family."

Connie nodded and leaned closer. She had many fond memories of Liz. "It was. They're still mourning her. But

I'm not a replacement daughter. Although your father and
Liam have always treated me well, I'm still an employee."

He reached up and touched her cheek. "You're more
than that. You're like the glue that keeps everything together at the hotel. You single-handedly arranged Kieran's
wedding. I think they'd be lost without you."

Connie had always felt valued in her role at O'Sullivans,
but never more so than in that moment. Jonah's words
struck a chord, and she swallowed hard. "Thank you. For
understanding, I mean."

He swayed her a little and smiled. "And you *can* dance.
Maybe it's been your partners who had two left feet."

Connie smiled and was achingly disappointed when
the song ended and a faster tune started up. She asked to
sit down, and he complied immediately. They chatted for
a while, and when she excused herself to head to the bathroom, he stood politely and waited for her to leave. The
restrooms were toward the rear of the restaurant, down
a short passageway, and by the time she came out, there
were three men standing by the bar. Dressed in cowboy
gear, they were all tall and broad and had clearly been
drinking way too much. Connie felt their observation
as she approached and then cringed when the youngest
of the group made a crude comment. She held her head
steady, refusing to look down, remembering everything
she'd learned from the self-defense classes she'd taken.
She could handle a few drunken jerks at a restaurant. Be-
sides, she surely wasn't in any real danger. It was a busy
place, and no doubt she could have the manager or security at her side in a heartbeat if she made a scene. The
thing was, Connie didn't want a scene. She'd had all the
drama she could endure a decade ago and now liked her
quiet life and anonymity.

As she moved toward the table where Jonah waited,

one of the cowboys stepped sideways, halting her in her tracks.

"Hey, sweet thing," he drawled. "Can I buy you a drink?"

"No, thank you."

He smiled, reeking of liquor—and trying her patience. "No need to be unfriendly."

Connie exhaled. "Would you please let me pass?"

"In a minute," he drawled. "I'd like to talk to you for a while."

Connie's back straightened and she noticed his companions smirking. She was about to sidestep when he reached out and placed a hand on her shoulder. Her instincts surged. She grabbed his hand, twisting it around as she turned his arm in an arc until his back was turned and pushed his arm upward. He yelped, staggered and took a couple of steps forward until he landed against the bar.

She turned her foot, pressed her heel into the back of his knee and he dropped like a stone.

Chapter Five

Jonah watched the interaction unfold in slow motion as he wove through the tables and headed for the bar area. The moment he'd realized Connie was being harassed by the cowboys, he'd almost flown across the room. Still, he didn't make it in time and had to watch as Connie handled the jerk who was twice her size.

By the time he was at her side, the cowboy had staggered to his feet and she had stepped back, breathing heavily, her gray eyes wide and filled with a kind of panic that knocked the air from his lungs. He half shielded her, waited for the other man to turn around and then spoke.

"If you want to try that again, understand that if you do, next time you won't get back up."

The cowboy held up his hands. "I was only trying to be friendly and—"

"I know exactly what you were trying to do," Jonah said, keeping his voice low, aware that they were being watched and the manager was now making his way toward them. "Touch her again, and I will end you."

He heard Connie's sharp intake of breath behind him. Felt her shrink back even though they weren't touching. He wanted to turn on his heels and haul her into his arms and let her know that she had nothing to fear from him and that he would protect her with his last breath. He felt foolish thinking it, knowing there was no need for such dramatic behavior. But he would do it, just the same.

The manager arrived, alongside a security guard, and it took about half a minute to have the trio of cowboys escorted from the restaurant. He grasped Connie's elbow gently, felt her tense beneath his touch and then released her immediately. They returned to their table and he didn't say a word for a moment. She sipped her drink and he noticed her hands were shaking. Finally, he spoke.

"Are you okay?"

She nodded. "Fine."

"Where did you learn how to do that?"

She met his gaze. "Do what?"

"Take down someone twice your body weight."

She shrugged. "Self-defense classes."

He nodded, but he was surprised by her admission. "I'm sorry I didn't get there in time. I would have—"

"Ended him," she said, cutting him off. "Yes, I heard. You don't strike me as the bar-brawler type."

"I'll fight if I have to."

"Offense or defense?"

"Is there a difference?" he shot back.

"Absolutely," she replied. "The truth is, I can't stand violence. I don't watch violent movies or sports that advocate it."

Her tone had changed. She sounded angry. "I didn't

mean to upset you. And you appeared to have the situation under control."

She shrugged. "I'm amazed I remembered how to do it. I haven't been to a class in years."

Jonah looked at her. "It seemed to come back to you well enough. He dropped like a rock."

A shadow seemed to flicker over her face, and she wrapped her arms around herself. "Do you mind if we go now?"

"Of course not. If you're rattled by what happened I can call someone for you," he suggested gently. "A friend or—"

"I'm already with a friend," she said and smiled. "Right?"

Jonah's gut clenched. "Right."

A couple of minutes later, the check had been paid and they were heading from the restaurant. He lingered by the door for a moment, scanning the parking area, ensuring the jerks who'd harassed her were not loitering somewhere close by. When he realized the area was clear, they headed for the car. Jonah opened the passenger door and waited until she was buckled in before he walked around to the other side. She was noticeably quiet—and he was concerned.

"Are you sure you're okay, Connie?"

"Just a little shaken up. But I'll be fine."

"Don't let a few loudmouthed jerks upset you. Particularly since you handled them so well."

"I'm not proud of doing that," she said pointedly. "I don't like hurting people. Jerks or not."

"They deserved it."

"Doesn't make it right."

Jonah started the ignition. "Then why did you do it?"

"Instinct," she replied. "Self-preservation."

"You did what you had to do."

She sighed. "Maybe. Anyway, thank you for a nice evening."

"It's not over yet."

She glanced sideways. "Do you have something else planned?"

"I thought we could have a drink at the hotel bar," he suggested. "Unless you're embarrassed to be seen with me?"

She laughed softly. "Not at all. I do live my own life, you know. But since we'd have to almost drive past my street to get there, how about you take me home instead?" she said and then raised a hand. "That's not an invitation to sleep over. Just coffee and conversation. And you can meet my dogs. They're the best judges of character that I know."

Jonah grinned and headed down the highway. "You think I need character judgment?"

"Not especially. In fact, I think your reputation is your disguise."

He laughed. "You won't tell, will you?"

"Your secret is safe with me," she replied. "Anyway, I think the O'Sullivans are smart enough to work it out for themselves."

"There's that blind faith again."

She made an impatient sound. "They're not your enemy, you know? If you'd give them a chance, you'd discover that they are all good people. Even your father."

Jonah flinched at the reference. "I'm sure he has his qualities."

"Would you like a list?" she shot back and then began tapping examples off her fingers. "Kindness. Consideration. Strength. And he's also generous."

"You forgot integrity and loyalty," Jonah suggested. "Oh, wait…those are probably not on the list."

"God, you're hard-nosed about some things."

"About J.D.?" he said and shrugged. "I suppose I am. Habit."

"Was he such a bad father?"

Jonah took a moment to reply, feeling the anxiety well in his gut. "He was mostly absent."

"But he didn't completely neglect you? I mean, he was there for some of your birthdays and graduations and all of those things."

"For some," he replied, not elaborating.

"Well, you're lucky… That's more than what I got from my folks."

"But you weren't their dirty little secret, were you?" he said, pushing back the familiar resentment churning through his blood. "I was."

"From all accounts, he wanted the truth to come out years ago and your mom didn't—"

"My mom did what was best for me," he said, harsher than he liked. "And she had too much respect for Gwen O'Sullivan to break up that family."

As he said the words, Jonah felt them through to his bones. He'd always believed his mother had done the right thing…the only thing. The part he couldn't under-stand was J.D.'s insistence that he stay connected to their lives. The other man should have left them alone. That would have been the kind, decent thing. Except J. D. O'Sullivan was so righteous and arrogant that he needed to be in control of everything…including the part-time family and secret he believed was rightfully his to hold on to. That's why Jonah hated him. And always would.

"I guess everyone did what they thought was right," Connie said quietly, and Jonah realized he didn't resent her opinion as much as he thought he would.

"Perhaps," he agreed. "It's all moot now, anyhow, since

the cat is completely out of the bag. My mom is back in Cedar River and everyone knows the whole sordid story."

"Still, it must be nice to be loved so much," she said and smiled.

He found himself chuckling. "Is your glass always half-full?"

"Yes," she replied. "And yours half-empty?"

He laughed. He liked that Connie didn't back down. She wasn't a pushover. Watching her bring that six-foot-something cowboy to his knees had made Jonah realize that even more. She was strong and resilient and not anyone's doormat.

"You're really something, you know that?"

"Thank you," she said quietly. "You're not so bad yourself."

Before he could respond, she asked him about the planned extension of the museum, and they talked about that for the remainder of the drive. When he pulled up outside her house, it was past ten. They got out, and as they headed through the gate, the sensor light on the porch flicked on. The dogs barked, then he heard the sound of paws rushing over floorboards.

"Sounds like quite the welcome-home committee," he said and stood back while she took out her keys and opened the door.

Before the hounds had a chance to escape, she commanded them to sit. They obeyed immediately, and she stepped aside and ushered him in. The dogs stayed where they were, noses in the air, sniffing madly. The smallest of the pack had a rumble low in its throat, the kind that was more cautionary than real threat.

"This is Ruffalo," she said and pointed to the tall wolfhound, then gestured to the smaller, shaggy white-and-gray pooch with one eye. "And this is Annabel. That's

Roger and the one growling is Mr. Jangles. But don't take offense…he doesn't generally like anyone except me."

"Thanks for the heads-up."

She smiled and Jonah's chest tightened. There was something intoxicating about her smile. She dropped her bag on the hall table and asked him to follow. Jonah did as she requested, waiting a moment as the dogs followed in her wake, clearly delighted that she was home. He looked around as they headed down the long hall. The house was old, but the floorboards were polished, and as they passed the living room he noticed the mix of antique and new furniture pieces. There was a small television and a pair of matching sofas and a large fireplace. When they entered the kitchen, he glanced around and smiled to himself. Cedar countertops, shaker-style cabinets, copper pots suspended from a timber grid above the counter, planters containing herbs by the long window— it was exactly how he'd imagined it would be. Neat, but homey and welcoming.

Jonah watched as she instructed the dogs to go to their beds, which were all lined up by the back door, and then she moved around the counter and pulled a couple of mugs from one of the overhead cupboards. Like with everything she did, she was methodical and efficient as she made coffee for him and tea for herself.

"Black," he said and perched on a stool on the opposite side of the countertop. "And sugar."

She placed the mug on the counter, and for the first time he noticed that her hand was shaking slightly. He met her gaze, saw the tension in her expression and recognized something that looked a lot like fear in her eyes.

"Are you afraid of me?"

She shook her head. "No."

"Then why do you look as though you think I'm about to pounce?"

She exhaled heavily and did a vague shrug. "Habit."

He frowned. "What does that mean?"

"Nothing," she replied quickly and came around the counter. "I'm probably still shaken up from what happened at the restaurant."

Jonah wasn't so sure, but he nodded. "You were safe, you know. I wouldn't have allowed them to hurt you."

She looked up sharply. "I know and thank you. But I can take care of myself."

"So I noticed," he said and sipped the coffee. "You've got quick reflexes."

"Better watch out, Rickard," she said and smiled a little, then her expression sobered. "Can I ask you something?"

He shrugged. "Sure."

"Why don't you have your father's name?"

It was about as personal as it got, and usually he'd shut down and refuse to reply. But he sensed that Connie wasn't going to let him dodge the question. "You know why."

"I can guess," she said quietly. "It hurts him, you know. If that's your intention."

"It's not about him," he replied. "It's about boundaries. Yes, J.D. *is* my biological father, but that's all he is. I don't care if it hurts him."

"And I don't believe you," she said flatly. "If you didn't care, you wouldn't hate him as much as you do."

"Reverse psychology?"

She shrugged. "Common sense. You're an emotional person. I can see why hating him is the easy option."

He sighed. Connie had a way of getting directly to the core of things. "I don't want to talk about J.D."

"Then what do you want to talk about?"

"Talking is overrated," he said and placed his mug on the counter.

She took a deep breath. "Is this the kissing part now?"

"The what?"

"You said you wanted to kiss me," she reminded him. "As part of the big date."

Jonah's gut did a leap. "I'm not going to swoop, if that's what worrying you."

"I'm not worried," she said quietly. "You don't seem the swooping type."

His mouth twisted. "There's a type?"

She shrugged. "Maybe. I'm not an expert on male behavior."

"Oh, I don't know about that," he said and stepped toward her, keeping a foot between them, waiting for her to retreat, and when she didn't, Jonah reached out and took her hand. "You've made your opinion of me abundantly clear since we first met."

"Because you've acted like a jerk most of the time."

"That's true," he said and turned her hand over, stroking her palm with his thumb. "But since we've already established that I'm growing on you…"

She smiled, and his insides clenched. She had a way of getting a reaction without doing anything overt, and it wreaked havoc with his common sense. Jonah didn't do that sort of stuff. When it came to women, he was level-headed and in control one hundred percent of the time. Except around Connie. He urged her a little closer, and when she didn't resist, he felt his blood heat.

"You are," she said softly. "Growing on me, I mean. But I want to be very clear about things, which means I'm not in the market for a broken heart, Jonah. So, before you make your move, just know that…okay?"

He swallowed hard, her honesty flooring him. "Okay… I hear you."

She nodded and sighed as Jonah moved his hand to her neck, stroking her nape with his fingertips. Her lips were parted slightly, her eyes wide and curious…and something else. Nervous, maybe. Jonah stared at her, looking over every feature, every curve and angle of her beautiful face.

"If you want me to leave, I will," he said quietly, keeping space between them.

"I know you will," she replied, sighing deeply. "That's what makes me want you to stay."

Jonah reached out to grasp her chin, gently tilting her face upward. "Did someone break your heart once, Connie?"

"My heart," she whispered, as though the memory hurt her down to her very core. "My spirit."

Jonah's insides crunched. "I understand caution when it comes to getting close to people," he said, rubbing his thumb across her cheek. "Sometimes I think I invented it. But I'm not out to hurt you or make empty promises. I just want—"

"Sex?" she said, cutting him off.

Heat smacked his cheeks, but he wasn't about to lie to her. "I'm a guy," he said and shrugged. "We're kind of programmed that way."

She laughed humorlessly. "At least you're honest about it."

"I don't lie, Connie," he said, more seriously. "I will always tell you the truth about my motives. It's obvious that I'm attracted to you and I think that's mutual…right?"

She nodded. "Yes."

"So, we'll just see where it goes."

"To bed, you mean?"

He shrugged again. "If that's what you want."

"And it's completely my decision?"

"Of course," he replied. "Always."

She took a moment to respond, and then nodded. "Okay."

"Okay?"

She nodded again. "Maybe we *will* end up in bed. We'll just have to see."

He smiled. "Is everything usually so cut-and-dried with you?"

"Usually," she replied. "We doormats are generally the boring, black-or-white type."

"I thought you'd forgiven me for that remark."

"I have," she said softly and moved closer. "I'm making fun of you." She looked up at him, meeting his gaze, her mouth slightly parted, her eyes wide. "You can kiss me now…I mean, if you still want to."

Jonah's entire body tensed. He wanted to. Very much. She was close, and when her breasts touched his chest it almost sent his libido into overdrive. Jonah took a breath, grasped her chin and hovered his mouth over hers. They'd kissed before, but somehow, being so close, hearing her breathe, inhaling the scent that was uniquely hers, Jonah experienced an acute sense of being in the moment, of feeling and sensing nothing else other than everything that was Connie. It should have set off alarm bells in his head. But instead, he felt the rightness of it through to his blood and then felt it seep deep into his bones. He was hooked. Totally at the mercy of his desire for her. With no foreseeable way out other than to make a run for it.

Which was out of the question.

Connie slipped her arms around his shoulders, feeling the muscles bunch beneath her fingers, feeling every part of him in a way that was impossibly intimate and breathtakingly scary. His eyes glittered brilliantly, meeting hers without blinking, holding her gaze with such burning intensity she could barely draw breath. They were breast to chest, thigh to thigh, and she waited for the usual panic to rise, for her old fears to make a comeback, for the memories to resurface and warn her off. But oddly, they didn't. Because she wasn't afraid of Jonah. She desired him. She liked him. She *trusted* him. And trust had always been in short supply in her life.

Strange, some faraway voice whispered to her, that she trusted Jonah without really knowing him very well. For Connie, trust was earned, and garnered by time and integrity and actions. She trusted Liam and J.D. because they had witnessed her at her most vulnerable and saved her from the worst moment in her life. She trusted her friends Annie and Nicola because they had never had a morbid curiosity about her past like some others had shown over the years. And that, she realized, was it.

Four people. A small circle of trust in any language.

And now, inexplicably, there was Jonah.

Crazy. Senseless. Potentially foolish, because he had so much emotional baggage that it was certainly going to end in disaster…or at the very least, her broken heart.

But when his mouth touched hers, she was gone. He softly coaxed her lips apart, gently anchoring her head with a steady palm at her nape. There was nothing rushed, nothing overpowering, nothing other than a gentle coax and a request for permission. She gave it instinctively, and when his tongue touched hers, Connie experienced a deep surge of desire spark through her veins. His kiss was something she would never get enough of. And there was no threat, no demand. He was *asking* for her to kiss him back, seeking her agreement to ensure that they were heading to the same place, a place that had always terrified her, because it meant absolute surrender.

And surrender meant vulnerability…something she'd vowed never to allow again.

Connie moaned, hearing the sound echo low in her chest, feeling the vibration through her blood and across every nerve ending. *It's just a kiss.* But it was more. That's what struck her the most. She'd been kissed before. She'd put herself out there and gone on several first dates…but never had a man's kiss affected her on a such a deep, sensory level. The fact that it was Jonah who wreaked such havoc with her senses…Jonah, who was in constant conflict with everyone she cared about the most, was confusing and contradictory to everything she thought she believed in.

But when his mouth touched hers again, when he deepened the kiss and his tongue danced with hers, she was utterly and categorically *undone*. She pressed closer, feeling him aroused against her, but she sensed no threat and no need to run. That's what shook her…that he wasn't a threat. That he would never be a threat. That she'd found a man who made her feel safe.

And she wanted him.

She wanted him in ways she'd never wanted anyone before.

But, like a cold bucket of reality washing over her, Connie realized that surrender to Jonah put her in grave danger. Because if she allowed herself to feel, he would *see* her. He'd learn her secrets.

"Jonah," she said against his mouth. "Please…stop."

He did so immediately, pulling back and releasing her. "Too soon?" he asked quietly, the pulse in his cheek throbbing faster than usual. His hands were at his sides and he took another step back, putting space between them.

Connie shook her head. "It's not that. You know I'm... You know that I *like* you. I'm just not good at—" she gestured between them "—this stuff."

His mouth curled at the edges, and he watched her with blistering intensity for a moment before he spoke again. "Are you a virgin?"

Connie bit back a gasp. God, did she appear so naive? So clumsy? So out of her depth? "Ah...no."

"How many lovers have you had?"

It was impossibly personal question. "Not as many as you, I'm sure."

He laughed softly. "I shouldn't have asked you that. But I'm trying to figure you out," he admitted and shrugged. "And failing."

"I don't mean to be complicated," she said quietly. "Or hot and cold. I *am* genuinely attracted to you. But I don't want to rush into anything. I don't rush...ever. Except that night with you at the hotel, I guess you could say I rushed...but it all happened so fast. And tonight... I had a nice time, which was unexpected and made me really confused. Because I like you and I'm not sure I can cope with it becoming anything more than that too quickly. Does that make sense?"

He nodded slowly. "It goes both ways, you know. You're not the only one who sucks at relationships. Would it surprise you to know that I've never had a proper girlfriend... I mean, someone who moves in or has a drawer in the dresser or leaves her toothbrush in the bathroom cabinet. So, we're both novices here. Do I want to make love to you? Absolutely," he said candidly. "But that's for you to decide. In the meantime, I'd also like to spend some more time with you. Just hanging out," he reassured her. "Can we spend the day together tomorrow?"

Connie's head reeled with shock at his bald honesty. He really didn't sugarcoat anything.

"I can't tomorrow."

He frowned. "Why not?"

"I'm helping Kieran and Nicola move," she explained. "You know they're moving into the O'Sullivan ranch and Gwen has relocated into town, right?"

He nodded. "Sure. And you'll be doing that all day?"

"I didn't set a time limit. Nicola is my friend and I said I would help." An idea formed. "Would you like to join me?"

She could have asked him if he'd like to chew glass and probably would have gotten a less scowling expression. He looked at her for a moment, his handsome head tilted to the side, his gorgeous mouth curled up. Then he spoke. "Sure…why not."

Connie raised both brows. "You do understand that it means spending the part of the day with the O'Sullivans? With your brothers? And possibly J.D.?"

He nodded. "How bad could it be?"

Connie laughed softly. "Knowing you… World War Three."

He chuckled. "I promise to be on my best behavior."

"Your best behavior," she said, a little sterner. "I have your word?"

"Yes," he promised.

"Even if Liam gets on your nerves or J.D. has the audacity to try to strike up a conversation?"

He didn't flinch. "Even then."

Connie smiled widely. "It's a date."

"Okay," he said. "And now, I should probably get out of here. I'll see you in the morning."

He kissed her, briefly and on the cheek, and then she watched him leave with a heavy feeling in the pit of her stomach. Tomorrow, she was going with him into O'Sullivan territory. It would be either her smartest move or the biggest mistake of her adult life.

Either way, Jonah Rickard had worked his way into her head.

And her heart.

Chapter Six

Jonah didn't have any illusions about his behavior. He'd agreed to hang out with the O'Sullivans because he wanted to spend time with Connie.

Still, driving toward the O'Sullivan ranch felt weird. He'd been there a couple of times before—for Kieran and Nicola's wedding and for Gwen O'Sullivan's birthday celebration—but he still experienced an uneasy tightening around the collar as he drove up the long driveway. Connie sat beside him, looking achingly pretty in jeans, a bright orange shirt and matching boots, and a short fur-lined coat. Her hair was loose and hung around her shoulders, and her face was free of makeup.

It's the freckles.

They were freaking adorable.

Jonah had discovered he liked freckles. A lot.

"Everything okay?" she asked as he drove around the

driveway and pulled up beside Liam's familiar black Silverado.

"Of course," he replied.

"I could have driven myself here," she said, repeating what she'd already said three times since he'd picked her up fifteen minutes earlier. "You know if we turn up together, everyone is going to think we're...you know..."

"What?" he queried, watching as color leached up her neck and hit her cheeks.

"You know...something."

Jonah half shrugged. "That's not exactly a lie, though, right? We are..." His words trailed off and he smiled. "Something."

"I have no idea what we are," she said and sighed. "You confuse me."

"I don't mean to."

"I know," she acknowledged. "Annoying, really. I think I'm definitely starting to like you."

"Just starting?" he teased.

She shrugged. "Okay... I *like* you. There... I said it. I like you a lot. Happy?"

He *was* happy. Being around Connie had a startling effect on his mood. She was like a tonic. When he was around her, everything else seemed way less complicated.

"It's mutual," he admitted.

She half laughed, half sighed. "Yeah, but you like me in a get-me-into-bed kind of way. And I..." Her words trailed off and she shrugged again. "We should go inside."

"Connie," Jonah said, more seriously. "Whatever you think I'm planning here, I'll always be up front about my motives. Yes, I think you're beautiful and sexy and I want you. But let's not overanalyze this thing. We're both adults, we're both single...we're not treading on anyone's toes here. And any opinions the O'Sullivans have don't matter one iota."

"They do to me," she said quietly. "Liam is my boss. You're his brother. That's got *complicated* written all over it."

"Then we'll say we're just friends," he said, irritation swiftly filling his chest. "And anything else is none of their damned business."

But he knew that wasn't quite true. She was right. The O'Sullivans would have an opinion. Because they had an opinion about *everything*. Particularly Liam and J.D.— Connie's two knights in shining armor. But Jonah didn't care what they thought. He liked Connie. He wanted to spend time with her. If they disapproved, to hell with them.

"But we're not just friends," she reminded him. "Are we? And we're not lovers, either."

Jonah reached out and grasped her chin, gently drawing her face to his. "We could remedy that."

She swallowed hard and he watched, fascinated, as her lips parted fractionally. She was both invitation and rebuttal—an intriguing mix that set his blood on fire. The thing was, Jonah suspected she didn't actually realize how intoxicating she was. How challenging. How mesmerizing.

She pulled back, and he dropped his hand. "So I can be another notch on your bedpost?"

"My bedpost doesn't have as many notches as you seem to think." He pulled the keys from the ignition and looked at her. "Don't always believe the worst of me, Connie."

"I don't," she admitted. "If I did, I wouldn't be here with you. In fact, I don't believe anyone sees who you really are...except perhaps your mom. You make me feel things and want things. But I'm not going to rush into anything, despite how much I might want to," she said and laughed softly. "I can't be someone I'm not. I don't know how to flirt or be sexy and seductive or play games. I'm not used to—"

"I'm glad you don't play games," he admitted. "Neither do I."

Jonah kissed her. Briefly. Soundly. Possessively. Because she was simply too damned beautiful to resist. And because he was tired of hearing her list everything she *wasn't*, when she was so much more. When he pulled back, she was panting hard, looking both startled and undeniably turned on. Then she smiled and nodded, as though she knew exactly why he'd kissed her.

"We should probably go inside," he suggested.

"Probably," she said on a sigh.

"You know, you might not think you're seductive or sexy," he said and touched her cheek. "But believe me, Connie, you are…very much so."

She smiled, turned in the seat and then gasped slightly. Jonah cranked his neck around and stared directly out the front window, and straight into the glowering and disapproving glare of his eldest brother.

"Looks like we're well and truly busted," he said and opened the door.

"Don't make things worse by getting into an argument," she demanded. "You promised to be on your best behavior, remember."

"I remember," Jonah replied. "But if he says anything out of line, I'll—"

"He won't," she assured him, grabbing her bag and coat before she quickly got out of the car.

Jonah lingered by the door for a moment while Connie walked toward Liam and spoke to him quietly. Jonah could guess what was said, and by the time he reached his half brother, Liam wasn't scowling quite as hard, but he still looked mad as hell.

"Morning," Jonah said so agreeably his teeth hurt.

"I didn't expect to see you here," Liam remarked.

Jonah's back straightened and he was about to return with some acid-laced reply when he caught Connie looking at him questioningly, both brows raised. He managed a light shrug. "I thought I'd help."

"That's very…generous of you," Liam said, looking suspicious. "I'm sure Kieran and Nicola will appreciate the extra hands."

"Haven't they heard of this great invention called a moving company?" Jonah shot back.

Liam's mouth curled at the edges. "Apparently Nicola is too thrifty to waste money on hiring professionals."

"Oh, stop whining, you two," Connie said and grinned, wrapping her arms into her coat. "It's not like you have to move a grand piano or anything heavy. Anyway, you both look strong enough to carry a few boxes. Where's Nicola and Kayla?"

"In the kitchen," Liam replied and then tapped Jonah on the shoulder. "You can come with me."

Jonah started to refuse, but Connie had quickly headed up the path and he was left with only his brother for company. "If you're going to get all alpha male and voice your opinion, I'd rather you do it sooner rather than later."

Liam didn't flinch. "If you think I disapprove, you're right."

"Thankfully Connie and I don't need your approval," Jonah replied. "So, where's this grand piano you were so concerned about?"

Liam made an impatient sound and pointed to a truck parked around the side of the house. "I care about Connie. We all do. And no one will stand idly by and watch her get hurt."

"I have no intention of injuring Connie in any way," he said and began walking.

Liam was beside him in three strides. "If you start something you don't intend to finish, that *will* hurt her."

Irritation coursed through his blood. But he remembered the promise he'd made Connie and took a long and defusing breath. "I know what I'm doing."

"Leading her on with false promises?" Liam queried. "Using her?"

"I'm not the one who treats her like an errand girl," Jonah said and kept the lid on his temper. "That's your department."

Liam was in his space in two seconds. "What does that mean?"

"Working on a Sunday? Babysitting? Picking up your dry cleaning?" He made a mocking sound. "Spare me the lecture about acceptable behavior. Not when you and J.D. treat her as though she's your private housemaid. If Connie was sensible, she'd tell you to go to hell and then ask for a huge raise."

Liam stared at him, frowned for a moment and then laughed loudly. "Oh, I see. You actually *like* her."

Jonah turned hot all over. He didn't enjoy being laughed at. And Liam was laughing…hard.

"Is that so difficult to believe?" he demanded.

Liam shrugged. "Not at all. Connie is a special woman. Just don't mess with her or you'll answer to me."

Now Jonah laughed. "She's very capable of taking care of herself. And making her own decisions. Although I am intrigued by your and J.D.'s constant need to protect her from the world."

"Habit," Liam said flippantly and pointed to the boxes

sitting on the edge of the truck's rear door and marked with the words *dining room*. "Let's start with those."

Jonah grabbed a box and walked off, circumnavigating the house to get away from his annoying half brother. He headed back up the front path and entered the house, shouldering his way through the front door and walking down the hallway and toward the dining room.

However, the room wasn't empty. Gwen O'Sullivan sat in a chair by the window, with Liam and Kayla's baby son cradled in her arms. He stalled in the doorway, aware that he'd been seen but suddenly wanting to make a run for it.

"Hello, Jonah," she said and beckoned him into the room. "It's okay, my grandson is fast asleep. I should probably place him in his bassinet," she said and smiled. "But I adore holding him."

"Hello, Mrs. O'Sullivan," he said and shrugged a little. "I'll just leave this box on the table."

He looked around the room. A few of the glass cabinets were empty, but other than that, the room appeared as stylish as it always had. Clearly Gwen O'Sullivan wasn't clearing the house of all her belongings.

"You really need to start calling me Gwen," she said and got to her feet, then gently placed the baby in the crib.

"I don't think I can do that."

She waved a hand. "Nonsense. I'm not your enemy, Jonah."

"I know," he replied. "You've always been very understanding."

She smiled. "You're not to blame for the way things worked out. And you didn't ask to be born into the middle of such a complicated situation." She glanced lovingly at the baby in the bassinet. "Children are innocent."

Jonah's chest tightened, and his respect for Gwen

O'Sullivan grew. She was quite a lady. "I'm not sure I'd be as generous if the situation was reversed."

"I think you would be," she replied. "I think you are mostly a rational and compassionate man. But you're angry with J.D., and those feelings can cloud a person's judgment. I understand, believe me," she added with a small and ironic smile.

Yes, he thought, she actually would. "He never deserved you."

She let out a brittle laugh. "Probably not. But love can also cloud a person's judgment. And J.D. does have his good qualities. He was, and still is, a caring father. Even to you," she added when she obviously picked up on Jonah's scowl. "He didn't abandon you or Kathleen. And he could have."

"I wish he had."

"No, you don't," she said quickly but gently. "If he had, you might not be here now. And as hard as this situation is for you...for us all...I believe that with time and effort, everyone's life will be richer for having you in it."

It was, he realized, one of the kindest and most sincere things anyone had ever said to him. Jonah's throat thickened and he swallowed hard, trying to find the words to reply. But Gwen spoke before him.

"I've had to learn how to forgive him," she said and sighed. "Otherwise, I would get bogged down in resentment and bitterness. And that's not the way for anyone to live their life, is it?"

Jonah's back straightened. "Is that a question?"

She half shrugged. "Not really. I imagine the last thing you need is another person dishing out advice."

She was right and he appreciated her voicing the fact. "Thank you."

Gwen smiled. "Can you watch over the baby for a moment? I need to speak with my daughter-in-law."

Jonah glanced at the crib and shrugged. "Yeah...sure."

She nodded and left the room. Once she was gone, Jonah walked toward the window and stared out. He watched as Liam and Kieran stood together, laughing at something one of them said. He wondered if he'd ever have that with them. Camaraderie. Caring. A relationship that came from sharing DNA and genuine affection.

The baby stirred, making a soft but unhappy sound, and Jonah headed for the crib. Jack's eyes were closed, but tears were plumped at the corners, and before Jonah could make a soothing sound, the baby let out an unholy wail and waved his tiny arms. He gently touched the baby's head, and when that made no difference, he lifted the infant from the crib. The wailing stopped instantly.

Right. He was holding a baby. Jonah settled the child into the crook of his arm and stared at him. He was cute. It was the first time he'd looked at Jack and made the connection that the baby was his nephew. His blood. Being an only child, Jonah had never imagined he'd be an uncle. But as he stared into Jack's now peaceful face, he liked the idea.

"You know, that look really suits you."

Connie.

Jonah turned and spotted her standing in the doorway, arms crossed, her expression soft.

He glanced at the baby. "Do you think?"

She smiled and walked into the room. "Gwen said she'd left you with babysitting duty, and I thought I'd come and help. But," she said and came up beside him, "you don't look like you need any help."

"Until there's a diaper change," he said with a mock grimace. "Then he's all yours."

She chuckled. "I'm sure you'd manage," she said and stroked the baby's cheek. "God, he's so precious. I envy them," she said on a sigh. "Your brother and Kayla. They worked through a lot of stuff to get to this point. But I reckon this little guy was worth every moment."

"Is that your clock I can hear ticking?" he teased.

She shrugged. "Maybe. I think I would like children someday. If I can find someone who'd be able to put up with me. I mean, you did say I was high-maintenance."

He laughed. "I did. You are. But not in a bad way. Incidentally, Liam gave me a lecture outside."

"I figured he would."

"He said it was habit that put him into protective mode around you," Jonah remarked. "What does he mean by that?"

She looked at the baby. "You'd have to ask him."

"I'm asking you."

She shrugged. "Just Liam being Liam. You know how he gets."

"Protective and overbearing?" He nodded. "Yeah, I get it. I just don't understand why he feels the need to be that way toward you."

She looked up. "You shouldn't let it bug you."

"Maybe I shouldn't," he quipped. "But it does. They all act like they have some claim on your affections and your life. I'm just trying to figure out why."

She stepped back. "There's nothing to figure out. They've known me since I was a teenager."

Jonah wasn't convinced it was something that simple. "Have you ever been romantically involved with any of my half brothers?"

Connie's patience was wearing thin. The man was relentless. She propped her hands on her hips and glared at him. "Of course not."

"So you're like a little sister to them all?"

"Exactly," she replied and sighed loudly. "Let up on this, will you?"

His mouth lifted at the edges. "You're angry because I'm curious. And yet, you don't hold back when telling me how I should behave. It goes both ways, Connie. Or at least, it should, don't you think?"

He had a point. A good one. But she wasn't about to start answering questions about her relationship with his family. Jonah didn't need to know about her past. They were in the present. And in the present, she thought he was the most attractive man she'd ever met. End of story. Of course, he was also the most infuriating.

"I'm an open book," she said, fibbing more than she liked.

"No," he said quietly and rocked the baby. "You're not."

Watching him with the infant made her heart ache with a longing she'd never imagined. Of course she'd often thought about having children. But the idea usually got overshadowed by memories of the past and her fear that she'd never trust anyone enough to make that kind of life-changing commitment. But seeing Jonah hold Jack made her toes curl, and somehow her lingering resistance began to fade away.

"Do you want kids?" she asked bluntly.

He looked at her. "I'm not sure. If I met the right person, maybe. I'm not exactly the poster child for the average kind of family."

"Who is?" she shot back. "My folks didn't want to be parents because it interrupted their careers, so they literally dumped me with my grandparents. You had a devoted mom and a father who *didn't* abandon you... Let's see...who had the better deal?"

His mouth curled at the edges. "You make a valid point. I have been lucky. My mother is amazing."

"And J.D.? Doesn't he get *any* credit for supporting you and your mom?"

"Money was never what I wanted."

"Do you think he should have left his wife and family to be with you and your mom?"

He inhaled sharply. "No. I wanted him out of our lives. I still do."

"And yet, you agreed to come here with me today," she reminded him. "The world hasn't ended. Maybe things haven't turned out so bad, after all. By the way, your dad's outside. Remember that you promised you wouldn't make a scene today."

He stared at her. "Are you enjoying telling me what to do?"

"Yes," she shot back. "Very much. I think you've been allowed to say whatever you want and get your own way far too much for most of your life."

"Is this the part when you call me a spoiled brat?"

She shrugged. "If the shoe fits. Be nice to your father, Jonah…he's the only one you have. Life is too short to be unforgiving."

"And you know this from experience?"

She nodded, feeling a heavy ache deep in her chest. Sometimes the memories of that awful day were acute. And other days it was as though it had happened to someone else and she felt almost…normal. "Just because I don't express every emotion I'm feeling every time I feel it, don't dismiss my opinion."

"I'm not. In fact, I respect your opinion a great deal, Connie. And I respect you."

She knew that about him. Jonah wasn't the kind of man to waste energy on saying things he didn't mean.

"That still doesn't let you off the hook—you have to be civil to J.D. For everyone's sake, including your own."

"I'll try," he said and shrugged and then gently laid a sleeping Jack back into his crib.

He also got the chance to see his father, because at that moment, the man himself appeared in the doorway. J.D. looked ruddier in the face than usual, and Connie experienced a pang of concern for the older man. Since his family had imploded, Connie had seen a significant change in him. He looked old. Tired. She was becoming genuinely concerned for his health.

"Can I have a word with you, son?" J.D. asked as he hovered in the doorway.

Connie saw Jonah scowl at the *son* reference and lightly jabbed him in the ribs with her elbow, ignoring the way a shot of electricity raced up her arm at the connection. "I'll just leave you two alone so you can—"

"Stay," Jonah urged quietly. "I insist."

Connie sighed, stepped back and crossed her arms. "Okay."

"What do you want?" he asked J.D. coolly.

His father took a few steps into the room. "I wanted your advice on something," he said and moved around the table.

"What kind of advice?"

"Business. There's an old warehouse down by the river that's been empty for a few years," J.D. said quickly. "I've never really known what to do with the place. I was hoping you'd have some time to take a look at it. It needs some renovation work before it goes on the market. Or, alternatively, we could pull the place down and build something new."

"Something new?"

J.D. nodded. "I'd like to get your professional opinion, you know, if you think it's worth a remodel."

"I don't have time to—"

"He'd love to," Connie said, cutting through Jonah's refusal. "Wouldn't you?"

To his credit he didn't scowl. But she knew he was mad. The tiny pulse in his check throbbed wildly. But she wasn't put off. Connie cared about J.D.—and she cared about Jonah, too. Someone, she realized, needed to act as envoy between the two men. And since she was in the middle of them, it might as well be her.

"Sure," he said, his expression telling her she was going to have to explain her blatant interference at some point. "I'll catch up with you Monday morning before I fly back to Portland."

The older man nodded and winked at Connie. "Thank you."

"What are you doing here anyway?" Jonah asked bluntly. "I can't imagine Gwen wants you here."

"Just picking up the last of my things," he replied and then sighed. "My ex-wife and I can at least be civil with each other now."

"So the divorce is final?"

J.D. nodded. "It was uncontested, and both Gwen and I agreed on the terms."

"I'm sorry," Jonah said unexpectedly, and Connie saw J.D.'s eyes brighten a fraction. "I guess it's not easy to say goodbye to a thirty-five-year marriage."

"Easy?" J.D. shook his head. "No. But for best, considering." He glanced toward the crib and smiled wearily. "Gwen and I share grandchildren—for that reason alone, there's no point in being at war with one another. Family should stick together."

Connie didn't miss the point of J.D.'s words. Neither,

she suspected, did Jonah. But he remained silent until his father said goodbye and then left the room.

"You really shouldn't have done that," he said quietly.

"Done what?" she shot back. "Force you to spend time with your dad?"

"Stop calling him that."

"Why?" she queried. "It's who he is. J.D. is your father. You are his son. Stop being a horse's ass and just accept it."

"I can't," he said with more vulnerability than she expected.

Connie placed a hand on his arm, digging in, feeling him tense beneath her fingertips. "Sure you can. Take small steps and meet him halfway."

"It's not that simple," he said, looking to where her hand lay. "You don't understand how—"

"I understand that J.D. has tried over and over," she said, cutting him off. "I understand that he wants desperately to be a part of your life and you're too stubborn and selfish to let him in."

"I'm selfish?" he echoed incredulously and brushed off her hand. "Are you kidding? He's the one who had to have everything his own way. If he'd stopped coming around and trying to insinuate himself into our lives, then my mother might have met someone else. She might have had a chance at happiness."

Connie's insides suddenly ached for him. It was simplistic logic, a leftover remnant from a childhood filled with resentment and hurt. Feelings she knew well. But if the O'Sullivans were ever going to be a real family, with Jonah a part of that, then wounds had to be healed.

"She looks happy to me," Connie remarked, watching as he took a couple of strides around the room, suddenly restless and clearly not interested in continuing the conversation.

He jerked around and glared at her, keeping his voice low. "You weren't there. You weren't around when I could hear her crying at night after J.D. turned up for a visit. He'd give us a couple of days' notice that he was coming and she'd be on edge the whole time."

"That's to be expected, considering the circumstances," she said gently. "But he clearly wanted to spend time with you. Why do you hate him for that?"

"Because it wasn't enough," he admitted rawly. "And at the same time, it was too much. He'd make some weak effort at bonding, and all the time I was thinking, *Why can't he just stay the hell away from me and let Mom get on with her life?* And she never complained. She never asked for more. Every time she tried to explain to me how things were, how he had other responsibilities and another life far away, but how he was good to us and cared about us, I knew it hurt her deeply. And there was nothing I could do about it. Nothing I could say to make her stop hurting. I hated him for that. I still do."

Connie chose her words carefully. "I understand what you're saying, but if your mother chose not to move on because of her feelings for J.D., then that probably wouldn't have changed if he'd stopped coming to see you. In fact, maybe seeing him every now and then was all she needed."

"She wasn't happy," he shot back. "It wasn't all she needed. She needed someone who was there for her full-time. Not someone who was committed to another woman and his *real* family."

And there, she thought sadly, was his hurt. "I'm sure J.D. did the best he could, considering the circumstances. Sometimes all we can do is our best."

"Like your parents did?" he asked cynically. "Why are you so eager to let people off the hook, Connie?"

"Because I think forgiveness is more powerful than anger and hatred."

"That's a naive view of things," he said and shook his head. "And although I admire your blind loyalty to the O'Sullivans, I'm not wired that way."

"It's not blind loyalty, Jonah. I care about them. And I care about…I care about…" Her words trailed off uncomfortably. Admitting she had fledgling feelings for him hadn't been in her plans when she'd agreed for him to come with her to the ranch. "I'll stay here with the baby if you want to get back to helping unload the truck."

He frowned. "This conversation isn't over, Connie."

"Until you can start behaving nicer toward J.D., then it is over," she said flatly. "And so are we."

His chest puffed out instantly. "Blackmail?"

"An incentive," she replied and sat down on a chair by the window. "For you to become a better son."

He didn't look happy. Not one bit. "Not going to happen."

She shrugged loosely, ignoring the way her heart raced. "Suit yourself. But I don't imagine you enjoy being thought of as a grumpy, unforgiving jerk."

"And I thought we were past this," he said impatiently.

"Obviously not." He began to walk away.

Connie got to her feet in a microsecond. "Seriously," she demanded. "You're giving up that easily?"

He stilled instantly and turned back to face her. "You're impossible."

"So are you," she said and a took a few steps closer, staring at him. "What are you afraid of, Jonah? That you'll figure out that your father and brothers are good people and you might actually like them? Would that be so terrible?"

"Yes."

The rawness in his voice undid her, and without thinking she reached for him, wrapping her arms around his waist and resting her head against his chest, feeling the rapid beat of his heart through his shirt. It took a couple of seconds, but then his arms came around her, settling on her hips, drawing her closer, and she sighed, feeling him relax a fraction.

"I'm not your enemy," she said softly. "And I'd like to be your friend."

"Why?" he said into her hair. "I'm a grumpy jerk."

Connie chuckled. "Seems that I like grumpy jerks."

She felt him smile. "Nobody ever accused you of having good taste."

She gripped him harder. "Promise me something? As difficult as it might get, remember what's at stake."

"And what's that?"

"Family," she said simply. "Your family. And they're good people…the best I've ever known. Don't throw that away because you're angry."

"I can't change who I am."

"Yes, you can," she assured him. "You can change. And you can forgive."

She looked up, met his gaze, felt the searing heat of their connection through to the marrow in her bones. There was rawness in his expression, and a startling vulnerability she suspected he never showed to anyone. The fact that he was showing it to her filled Connie with an inexplicable ache. The feelings she had for him amplified in that moment, and she was confused and more aware of him than she had ever been of anyone in her life. She had no idea why Jonah stirred her so deeply. For a decade she'd steered clear of powerful emotions. But her feelings for Jonah intensified every time they were together.

He kissed her softly, drawing a response that she gave without hesitation.

Because she was halfway in love with Jonah Rickard.

And at risk of falling the rest of the way.

Chapter Seven

"When you two are done canoodling," a deep voice said from behind them, "I'd like to remind you that there are still boxes waiting to be unloaded from the truck."

Connie felt, rather than heard, Jonah groan low in his throat. But he released her immediately and she stepped back. Liam stood a few feet away, arms crossed, and Kieran was beside him, smiling.

Embarrassed, she straightened her shirt and ran a clumsy hand down her hair. She spotted Kayla and Nicola a few feet behind their husbands and suspected she was in for an inquisition once the men left the room. Of course, they had already queried her when she'd first arrived with Jonah. She'd fobbed them off with a casual remark about helping unload boxes, but she knew her friends weren't fooled.

It took precisely half a minute for Jonah and his brothers to leave, and she quickly muttered something about making tea when the two other women stopped her from making an escape.

"Oh, no," Nicola said and grinned. "We want details."

"There's nothing to tell," she said and stepped back into the room, watching as Kayla made her way toward the crib to check on Jack.

"That was nothing?" Nicola inquired, brows up. "You were just making out with Jonah."

Connie colored from head to heels. "I was not."

Kayla turned and grinned. "Sure you were."

"We kissed," she explained hotly. "That's all."

"There's a difference?" Nicola asked.

Connie knew her friends weren't going to let her off the hook. "A big difference. We've become friends and I—"

"The only man I kiss like *that*," Nicola said, grinning, "is my husband."

"Ditto," Kayla said and smiled.

"That was not a *friendly* kind of kiss, Connie," Nicola said and rested against the table. "So, spill."

Connie took a long breath. "Okay… I kissed him. And yes, we're something. I'm not sure what. And before you ask, because I know you will," she said and held up a hand, "no, I haven't slept with him."

"Are you going to?" Nicola asked.

"I don't know," she replied honestly. "Maybe. Probably. I'm not sure what I'm doing. I don't really know much of anything when it comes to Jonah. I only know that I like him."

"Why?" Nicola queried and then shrugged. "I mean, I know he's attractive and successful and all that. But he's also…"

"I think what Nic is trying to say," Kayla put in when Nicola's words trailed off, "is that Jonah is hard work. I know he's my cousin and also my brother-in-law and I should be telling you I think it's great and wish you the best, but I wouldn't be your friend if I didn't also say you need to be careful. Jonah is—"

"Not what people think," Connie said, cutting her off. "Look, I know everyone thinks he's arrogant and moody and plain old unpleasant most of the time, but he's actually quite funny and nice and very sweet."

"Sweet?" Kayla echoed incredulously.

"Okay," she agreed, irritation suddenly seeping through her blood when she realized how quick everyone was to paint Jonah as some kind of ogre. "Maybe *sweet* isn't the right word. But he's much more agreeable than everyone seems to think. Didn't he help Kieran out with the pond at your old place?" she asked Nicola. "And I know he's drawing up the plans for the museum extension at way below his usual fee. And if you must know, he's working on something with J.D. next week. So, he's not as bad you all seem to think he is."

"I didn't mean to suggest he was," Kayla said gently. "I know Liam is trying to—"

"Perhaps that's the problem," Connie said, cutting through Kayla's words. "Everyone is so busy trying to get him to *fit* in, he's suffocated. Maybe Liam and Kieran should let him work it out in his own time and in his own way. I'm sure that if the roles were reversed, they'd be just as cautious about getting too close too soon."

She stared at her friends, realizing how impassioned she sounded. But she wasn't going to stand idly by and allow Jonah to be maligned.

"We didn't mean to upset you," Nicola said gently.

Connie sighed. "I know."

"We just care about you and don't want to see you get hurt."

"Jonah would never hurt me," she said candidly. "At least, not intentionally."

Nicola didn't look convinced. "Will you at least promise to tread carefully? After everything you've been through, I just think—"

"I'm not made of glass," she said and pushed back her shoulders. "I know a lot of people think I'm fragile. But I'm not. I'm going to make tea," she said and left the room, leaving the two other women staring after her.

When she entered the kitchen, Gwen was by the counter, stacking up a pile of cookbooks.

"Everything all right, Connie?" she asked.

She nodded. "Fine. I was going to make tea."

"I've already put water in the kettle," Gwen remarked. "We have some time if you need to talk."

She ignored the offer. "It must be hard for you to leave this house."

"Not really," Gwen replied. "I have made countless wonderful memories here, but now it's time for new memories, for a new family to move in and fill the place with happiness. I know Kieran and Nicola and her nephews will do that. And I'm looking forward to having my own place in town. I'll be closer to the hospital where I volunteer, and I have many friends who live close by. It's certainly going to be an adjustment, but I'm looking forward to it. I've been rattling around in this big house on my own for way too long."

Connie knew Gwen had kicked J.D. out the day she'd found out about her husband's affair with Kathleen and his secret family. And through it all, the older woman had shown grace and humility and kindness, particularly toward Jonah.

Connie plopped into a chair, figuring she needed a

friend in that moment. "Why do you think everyone is so eager to think badly of Jonah?" she asked and sighed.

Gwen stopped what she was doing and turned. "Because he's the interloper," the older woman replied and then waved a hand. "And of course that's not true. But he clearly sees himself that way. He grew up an only child, quite possibly a loner, and now he's determined to play the role of the outsider looking in from the fringes of this family. I can't deny that learning about his existence was a shock for us all. Everything imploded when Liam and Kayla fell in love, and now Jonah is very much a part of our lives no matter how much he tries to keep us at a distance. Thinking badly of someone is often the easy option."

"But you don't," Connie said simply. "And you have more reason to resent his existence than anyone."

Gwen sighed. "You can't put an old head on young shoulders."

Connie understood the platitude and nodded. "He's not what people think."

"Most of us aren't," Gwen said. "You know how Liam has a reputation for being a hardnose and more interested in money than anything else. Then you see him holding Jack and know he's really just mush inside. And J.D.," she said and shrugged. "My ex-husband has always been considered to be blustering and overopinionated, but that's not entirely true. J.D. certainly has his flaws, but he's always been a good provider and caring father. And I believe he did try to be a presence in Jonah's life as the best he could considering the circumstances. As for Jonah…he is simply trying to find his place among a group of strangers he's connected to by blood. And he will," Gwen assured her gently. "If you can help him do that, I think it would be a good thing."

Connie didn't disguise her surprise. "So, you're not going to tell me I'm out of my mind for getting involved with him?"

"Of course not," Gwen replied. "You're a grown woman. Just take time to get to know him before you jump too fast."

"You mean before I jump into bed with him?" Connie queried, heat smacking her cheeks. "I think it's obvious that I'm not the jumping type."

"Understandable," Gwen said quietly.

Connie nodded fractionally. "I've never had a real relationship," she admitted, embarrassed yet oddly comforted by the older woman's counsel. "I guess you know that."

Gwen smiled and then her expression changed to concern. "Have you told Jonah about your past?"

"No," she replied quickly. "And I don't want him to know. I can't let my past define my present. Or my future."

"Our experiences always define us, Connie," Gwen said gently. "And if I've learned anything from this past year, it's that the truth is always best told."

As she made tea, using some of the bone china that Gwen had decided to leave at the house, and headed back to the dining room carrying a tray, she thought about Gwen's words. In her heart she knew the truth was best brought out into the open, but she had her reasons for wanting her past to remain exactly that. She didn't want the questions. The concern. The pity. And then the inevitable goodbye.

When she entered the room she saw that Kayla was feeding the baby, and Nicola was chatting about her two nephews, who were spending the day with Nicola's elderly father. It took about two minutes in their company for Connie's envy to kick in. It seemed she'd been thinking about babies a lot recently. And relationships. And commitment. And sex.

And all of it with Jonah Rickard.

She stayed for a while, long enough to sip half a cup of tea, and then she left her friends to find him. He was upstairs in one of the bedrooms, on a ladder, concentrating hard on hanging an airplane mobile from the ceiling. His shirt had pulled free from the waistband of his jeans, and when Connie caught a glimpse of his washboard abs, her libido, dormant for so long, rocked like a quake on the Richter scale.

She'd experienced desire before. She'd wanted someone's touch. But not like this. Jonah had tapped into the part of herself she wasn't sure even existed, since every time she'd gotten close to real intimacy with a man, she'd panicked and bailed. That night in Jonah's hotel room was the closest she'd ever been to making love with someone. Fear had made her run. But she wasn't afraid of Jonah, not anymore, not now that she knew him. As she watched him, as she allowed her gaze to follow every angle of his body, her old fears seemed like a distant memory.

"Jonah," she said softly.

He turned his head, saw her standing by the door and his expression softened. She loved how that happened, was thrilled by the way his scowl seemed to disappear when they were together.

"Hey," he said and continued to work on the mobile. "What have you been up to?"

"Girl talk," she replied and stepped into the room.

"It figures. My ears were burning," he said and grinned.

She laughed. "How did you get stuck with this job?"

"I volunteered," he replied. "Anything to get away from Liam barking out orders like a drill sergeant."

"I'm surprised you didn't tell him to go to hell," she quipped and walked around the room.

"Who says I didn't?" he replied and continued his task.

Connie laughed again. "Jonah?"

He looked back down and met her gaze, their visual connection brilliantly intense. "Yeah?"

Connie swallowed hard, felt her fears rise and then pushed them back. "I want…" She stopped, her words trailing off, her courage dwindling. Then she took a breath and continued, "I want you to make love to me."

Jonah almost toppled off the ladder. He blinked hard and met her eyes, their smoky depths undoing him.

"Ah…right now?"

She smiled and looked around the room. "No…but sometime."

There was color in her cheeks, and it registered in some part of his brain—the part that wasn't driven by his groin—that they were difficult words for her. There was an innocence about Connie, a kind of naïveté that suggested she wasn't very experienced. It was why he'd asked if she was a virgin. He'd stayed away from girls like Connie since college, sensing they expected more commitment than he was prepared to give. And back then he would have avoided a woman as inexperienced as Connie Bedford like the plague. But he wasn't about to avoid her now. He wanted her. It was chemistry. And she clearly felt the same way.

He finished hanging the mobile and stepped down the ladder. "Let's do something tonight."

"Are you asking me out on another date?"

He nodded. "No dancing shoes this time. Just you and me, a bottle of wine and somewhere quiet."

He watched, fascinated as she swallowed and her

lovely throat convulsed nervously. "Do you have some-where in mind?"

"My apartment," he supplied. "I'll cook."

Her brows came up. "You're cooking?"

"Not a chance," he said and grinned. "I'll order it from the hotel and heat it up later. No good having all this O'Sullivan DNA if I can't use it to my advantage every now and then."

She smiled warmly. "I'd like that."

"Now, get out of here before I forget my good inten-tions and kiss you."

She laughed but did leave, and he felt her absence like a blow to the gut. It was a feeling that had grown on him over the last few occasions they'd been together. Like leaving her got harder every time he had to do it. Once they were lovers, once he'd rid himself of the aching need he had to possess her, Jonah was sure the feeling would wane. It was only lust, he assured himself. Plain old sex-ual attraction. So, maybe this was more intense than he'd experienced before. Maybe he did enjoy spending time with her and hearing her voice and inhaling the scent of the fragrance she wore and how it seemed to linger on his clothes long after they'd parted company. *It didn't mean anything.* He wasn't the type of guy to get bogged down in feelings.

He wanted to get laid. He wanted Connie. It was sim-ple. And he intended to keep it that way.

By the time he headed back downstairs, there were more boxes to unload, and he spent another hour help-ing out. When lunch that had been provided by Nicola from JoJo's was ready, everyone hung out in the kitchen, and rather than experience an acute sense of exclusion, Jonah actually enjoyed the camaraderie he witnessed between Liam and Kieran and how they openly dissed one another, even pointing a few barbs in his direction. It was all in good humor and he wasn't fazed, no doubt because Connie was close by, her presence calming him, making it easier for him to relax, somehow, to be a part of the O'Sullivan clan.

And of course he didn't really dislike them. Kieran was easily one of the nicest people he'd ever met, and if they'd become acquainted under different circumstances, Jonah was certain they would have become friends. Liam was just *Liam*. In charge. Bossy. And quite likable in his own way. And Gwen was a kind woman who made him feel welcome among her family.

And there was Connie.

A rock. An ally.

And soon she would be his lover.

He dismissed the thought once they returned to the unpacking, and by three o'clock they were done. Kieran slapped him on the back affectionately and Liam shook his hand, and by the time he was driving from the ranch, with Connie in the seat beside him, Jonah felt relaxed and oddly happy.

"That wasn't so bad, was it?" she asked.

"Which part?" he teased. "The part where you made me talk to J.D.? Or where I was the butt of Liam's jokes?"

"You seemed to handle it okay," she said and smiled. "You're a tough guy—you can handle a little criticism."

"I've had lots of practice," he said and grinned. "After hanging around you."

She laughed and the sound hit directly in the center of his chest. He loved her laugh. It pierced him through to the core and made him feel lighter, less weighed down by the burden of Cedar River and all the place represented. He dropped her at home with a perfunctory kiss on the cheek, and they arranged for her to be at his apartment at seven. Then he headed into town and to the hotel.

Half an hour later he was hanging around near the kitchen waiting for his order when J.D. walked up behind him. The restaurant was closed, getting ready for the dinner service, but the chef had happily taken his order. But seeing J.D., as always, made Jonah's hackles rise. He pushed them back immediately.

"Twice in one day," the older man remarked. "It's good to see you again. What are you doing here?"

He pointed to the kitchen. "Ordering an early dinner. Which I paid for, in case you think I'm here to score a freebie meal."

J.D. moved beside him and frowned. "You can have whatever you want. This place is as much yours as it is Liam's, Kieran's and Sean's."

Jonah stilled. "Hardly."

J.D. shrugged. "I have four sons, and when I pass on, my estate will get split evenly."

"I don't want your money," he said tightly, wishing his dinner order would magically appear, cursing himself for not going to JoJo's for a pizza instead. "I don't want anything from you."

"I know," J.D. said wearily. "But you'll get it anyway."

Jonah pushed back his building rage. "Why can't you just leave me alone?"

"Because you're my son," J.D. said quietly and then paused when a waitress approached carrying a bag with Jonah's food. She said hello to them both, smiled and then disappeared back into the kitchen. Once she was out of sight, J.D. laid a hand on Jonah's shoulder and spoke. "That looks like dinner for two."

"It is," he replied coolly.

J.D. nodded. "Connie, I suppose. Tread carefully with her, Jonah. That girl has been through enough in her life."

Jonah's temperature soared. He had no interest in discussing his relationship with Connie with J.D.—not in any lifetime. "It's none of your business. And what the hell does that mean anyway?"

J.D. shook his head. "It's not my tale to tell. Just don't make promises you can't keep."

"Don't be like you, you mean," he said and made a dismissive sound. "Believe me, I have no intention of ever being anything like you. I saw my mom go through enough at your hands."

"I cared deeply about your mother. I still—"

"You care about yourself," he lashed out. "Let's face it, J.D., you are a screwup when it comes to things like integrity and honesty. That's not a legacy I intend on imitating. And my relationship with Connie is none of your damned business."

"That's true," he said, suddenly looking older than Jonah had ever seen him. "But I'm saying this out of concern for you, too. I know that you don't think I love you as much as I do your brothers."

Jonah's rage festered. He didn't want to hear it. "I don't care what you think."

J.D. sighed heavily. "I can assure you, son, that the truth is quite the opposite."

Enraged, he grabbed the food and left, trying to calm his heart rate as he left the hotel and headed home. By the time he got back to his apartment, he was calmer. He took a shower, as cold as he could stand, and then got dressed. He grabbed a bottle of wine from the rack by the pantry, collected everything he needed and made his way outside.

Damn J.D. for ruining his mood.

It's not my tale to tell...

Jonah had no idea what that meant. But he intended to find out.

By the time she drove to Jonah's that evening, Connie was so nervous her hands were sweating on the steering wheel. Once she pulled up outside the old Victorian, she grabbed her tote and smoothed her sweater down over her jeans, quickly pushed her arms into her wool coat and curled her scarf around her neck. It was dark out, but she could see the lights twinkling from the gazebo out back. Jonah had texted her an hour earlier, saying they were having dinner in the gazebo at the rear of the house, and she was delighted when she spotted lights dotted on the path. He was a romantic at heart, she realized, and almost swooned when she saw him by the structure, dressed in khakis, a white shirt and lined sheepskin coat. She saw the glow of a brass fire pit and realized he'd thought of everything. They spot was secluded and private and perfect as a prelude to a romantic and intimate evening.

"You look beautiful," he said when she reached him, taking her hand and raising her knuckles to his lips.

"You don't look so bad yourself."

He grinned, led her up the gazebo, and they sat at the small table. She heard music, something soft and dreamy and perfect for such a romantic setting. No one had ever gone to such lengths to make a date so special for her before.

"Are you warm enough?" he asked as he poured some wine.

Connie glanced at the fire pit and nodded, touched by his consideration, and sipped the wine. "I'm as warm as toast. It's lovely here."

"I thought you'd like it," he said and grinned. "No annoying cowboys to spoil our evening."

Connie smiled. "I'm happy about that. I didn't realize you were such a romantic at heart."

"Guilty as charged," he said and laughed softly.

He suggested they eat before the food got cold, and within minutes they were digging into a plate of spaghetti and a basket of crusty herb bread.

"Good?" he asked and smiled.

"Fabulous."

"I'm glad you're here."

She nodded. "Me, too."

His gaze narrowed. "I saw J.D. at the hotel. He advised me not to get involved with you unless I'm serious."

Connie stopped eating, her fork hovering in midair. "And are you?"

"Serious?" He nodded. "About you? Yes. Are you?"

"Of course."

He inhaled, placed his fork on the table and linked his fingers together. "Then maybe you can tell me what's going on with you...why J.D. said you had a tale to tell."

She shuddered and hoped he didn't notice. "I don't know what you mean."

"It's what J.D. said. Connie, have you been married? Divorced?" He hesitated. "Widowed?"

Connie's nerves frayed. "No to all of those things."

"You once said you'd had your heart and your spirit broken," he reminded her. "You also said the O'Sullivans saved your life. What did you mean by that?"

"I told you," she said quickly. "I was young, my parents had left town, your father gave me a job at the hotel."

He didn't look convinced. "And that's all?"

Connie hated lying. But for ten years, she'd been forced to live a lie by omission, by putting that time from her mind. And still, a decade on, she felt defined by that terrible day, as much as she'd tried to move on, to build a life for herself.

But it was hard.

Like now. When faced with her truth. When she had to look into Jonah's eyes and deny her past. "I can't tell you," she whispered.

His gaze narrowed instantly, and he reached across the table and grasped her hand. "You can. Whatever you say to me, it stays with me."

"It's not a secret, Jonah. It's just in the past, and that's where I'd like it to stay."

He squeezed her fingertips. "What happened to you?"

Her insides crunched. "Why do you need to know? It doesn't change the fact that we're here together and I thought we'd—"

"You thought we'd what?" he asked. "Make love tonight? Is that really what you want?"

She swallowed hard. "Yes."

He released her hand. "Even though you look scared to death of the idea. And of me."

Connie straightened in the chair. "I'm not," she assured him. "I want this. I want you."

"I want you, too, Connie," he said and exhaled heavily. "But not with secrets between us. You know everything about me. You *demand* to know everything…and that's okay, because I understand. I hate secrets and you know why. I *was* a secret for thirty years. If we're going to do this, then we need to be honest with one another."

Connie's heart sank. It wasn't a truth she'd ever verbalized. Or ever wanted to. She wanted it hidden. Tucked away. So she could pretend it hadn't happened and her innocence and trust weren't stolen from her that day. But she knew Jonah was stubborn and relentless and would keep digging until he uncovered the truth. It would be better if she made it easy for him by ending things before they really began. Even if it meant breaking her heart in the process.

She got to her feet, her legs unsteady. "You want to know the truth about who I am? You want to figure out why I seem so inexperienced? Why I've never had a serious relationship? The real reason I bailed that night in your hotel room?" She took a breath, garnering her courage. "Come on, Jonah, you're a smart guy...surely you can read between the lines. You asked me out on a date tonight," she said and grabbed her tote, willing strength into her legs. "Well, here's a date for you," she said and rattled off eight numbers. "Ask around, look that up on the internet. You'll get all the information you need and learn everything about me—every intimate and private detail." She secured her coat around her shoulders. "And then see if you can handle it."

She turned, tears welling at the corner of her eyes, and then fled.

Chapter Eight

Jonah sat in the gazebo for close to an hour. He finished the wine, packed up the dishes and the barely touched food, and headed back to his apartment. What was supposed to have been an evening to remember was now one he desperately wanted to forget. He followed that with thirty minutes of staring at the blank computer screen, trying to decide if he really wanted to know everything there was to know about Connie.

In the end, he realized he did.

And it didn't take long.

Tabloid headlines. A violent assault. Names suppressed. Three high school seniors.

A fifteen-year-old girl.

By the time he finished reading, he was sick to his stomach.

She'd been found on the roadside after escaping her attackers. Beaten. Raped. Barely conscious.

And then the sickness abated and rage, unlike any he had ever known, filled his blood. His fists clenched instinctively and he paced around his apartment, using up his energy, trying to get his breathing under control, glancing every now and then at the damning computer screen, hating everything it represented.

Slowly the rage in his heart subsided and helplessness emerged, forcing him to sit down. Memories bombarded his thoughts, and every harsh thing he'd said to her rose up and settled into his chest with an aching, relentless shame. His eyes stung and he cursed the whole damned world for allowing it to happen to her.

He wanted to call her, to see her, to hold her in his arms and tell her no one would ever hurt her again. But he knew she wouldn't allow that. Connie was proud and strong and obviously resilient.

And he wanted her.

In his heart, deep in that place he let no one enter, Jonah suspected he always would.

Despite his inner voice telling him to call her and apologize for being an unmitigated idiot, he held off contacting her until the following morning. He sent her a text message at nine o'clock.

Can I see you today?

He waited for a reply, staring at his cell phone for close to fifteen minutes before it beeped with a message.

I'm at home making Thanksgiving cookies.

He texted back immediately.

I like cookies.

More waiting. But the next message had a smiling emoji attached to it.

I thought you might.

Jonah smiled, feeling about sixteen years old. Whatever was going on between them, he knew he didn't want it to be over.

See you soon.

He didn't get a reply. Instead, he waited an appropriate twenty minutes and then headed to her place. The dogs were by the fence to greet him when he arrived, barking madly before she appeared by the front door and opened the screen, dressed in jeans and a bright pink shirt, with a chef's apron wrapped around herself. Her hair was in a ponytail and she had fur-lined moccasins on her feet. And she had a wooden spoon in her hand.

The dogs stopped barking and he let himself into the yard. They scurried around him for a few moments before quickly losing interest. Jonah reached the bottom of the steps and looked up, meeting her gaze, feeling the connection hum between them.

"Can we talk?" he asked simply.

She nodded. "Come inside."

She didn't bother to wait for him and he quickly followed, closing the door and smiling as the dogs scampered around his legs to get in before him. He headed down the hall and into the kitchen and saw she had baking sheets lined up on the counter and several mixing bowls scattered around as well.

"Looks like quite the production line."

She smiled lightly. "I make cookies for the residents at the veterans' home near the hospital."

His admiration spiked. She was, he realized, damned near perfect. Jonah moved around the counter and held his palms out. "What can I do to help?"

She shimmied sideways. "Mix this," she instructed and passed him a spatula and a bowl filled with an array of ingredients.

He began mixing and took a heavy breath. "I'm sorry that happened to you, Connie."

Her hand stilled for a second before she got back to her task. "You saw the reports?"

"Some," he replied. "But I'd like to hear it from you, if you're prepared to talk about it."

"I'm not," she said quietly. "I mean, I haven't talked about it since it happened, not really. But I will," she said and glanced sideways. "For you."

Jonah realized he'd been holding his breath, and he exhaled. "Thank you."

Twenty minutes later the cookies were in the oven, the trays cleared away and she had made coffee for him and tea for herself. He waited by the table while she completed the tasks, noticing everything about her. Like how she bit her top lip when she was thinking. Or how she had the most incredibly long lashes that fanned her cheeks when her eyes fluttered downward.

She sat at the table and he joined her. Her hands were clenched; she twisted them nervously and he longed to reach out and touch her. But he held back, waiting for her to speak. And finally, after several agonizing minutes, she did.

"I was fifteen," she said and shrugged. "A book nerd. I wanted to be a veterinarian and save all the animals. And one day I stayed late after math class and decided to take a shortcut home across the football field. There'd been a game that day, with another school out of state. Our school had won, and I didn't know that some of the players from the other school had been drinking under the bleachers." She stopped, took a breath, seemed to take strength from the air in her lungs and then continued. "Before that day I was naive, you know. I knew about sex, but only from books and what I heard other girls talking about at lunchtime or when they'd gossip about boys they liked in the girls' bathroom. I'd never even been kissed."

She hesitated again. "The odd thing was, I knew, even before they grabbed me, that something bad was going to happen. They had a look in their eyes…and it wasn't because they were drunk and out of control…this was something else. Like they'd been waiting for someone… anyone to come along. And that someone was me. I tried to fight…but they were strong and older and I didn't have any way of stopping them."

She took a breath, this one a shudder, and it made him ache inside.

"It's strange, but it was as though I had this feeling of disconnect through the whole thing. I can remember them ripping my clothes off. I can remember being naked and them being on top of me. Of feeling suffocated. Of being out of control. Of being powerless. But my mind went somewhere else… I had to… I think that was for the sake of my sanity. I remember thinking I was going to die on that field, beneath those bleachers, and that I'd never see my grandparents again, I'd never go to college, I'd never fall in love or get married or have children. And thinking about all the things I would never do made me determined not to die. I screamed and I screamed, but they put their hands on my mouth, and one of them put his hands around my neck and started squeezing."

There were tears in her eyes, and Jonah felt the backs of his eyes burn. But he blinked them away, determined to be strong for her. "Go on," he prompted gently.

"And from someplace, some faraway place in my mind, I knew I had to find the strength to get away. I kneed one of them, and I scratched and I kicked and I did everything I could to get them off me...and it worked. I had a chance—I found myself on my knees and then my feet and suddenly I was running. I was running so hard and didn't even feel the ground, even when the grass turned to gravel. They were drunk, so I guess they didn't bother coming after me. By the time I got to the road, I was hurting everywhere. And then I collapsed and passed out." She took another long breath. "I remember hearing a car. I remember feeling the vibration on the road. I remember voices. Male voices. And I remember thinking they'd come after me anyway, that they'd found me. This voice started speaking to me, telling me I was safe, that I was going to be okay. And I heard another voice... younger...but gentle. And then I felt a blanket around me...it was scratchy and made my nose itch. And then I was in a car and the rest is hazy.

"There was the hospital," she said and sipped her tea, her hands shaking so much Jonah reached out to steady her. At his touch she flinched, then relaxed. "The police came and asked me questions. They took swabs and did tests and gave me medication so I wouldn't get pregnant." Her voice cracked. "My grandparents came... I could hear them crying in the corridor. I was pretty badly beaten up, so I couldn't really talk properly for the first few days."

Jonah's chest was so tight he could barely breathe. "And the...individuals responsible?"

"The police found them," she replied. "They were

arrested and charged. The trial was held in another county to protect me from the media, and my name was never publicly released. But of course everyone in the town knew it was me… I couldn't go back to school… I couldn't walk around and see the pity and the ridicule. Kids can be cruel. So I left. I did homeschooling, got my degree and then went to work at the hotel. I did college online, too. I could have gone somewhere, but…I just didn't think I could cope with the campus and the football field and the corridors," she said, and he could see the admission cost her. "If that makes sense."

Jonah took the cup from her and then grasped her hands, holding them tightly within his own. "It does. Tell me about the two men who found you?"

"Can't you guess?" she said and managed a tiny smile.

Realization hit him. "J.D. and Liam."

She nodded and fresh tears glistened in her eyes. "They saved me. They protected me. They were there every day at the trial. Your dad made sure I didn't have to face them in court. He spoke on my behalf. And the prosecutor called them both as witnesses."

"There was a conviction?"

"Twenty-five years, not eligible for parole for the first eighteen." She sighed, clearly exhausted. "It was considered to be a particularly brutal attack, and because of my age they were sentenced accordingly."

Jonah had no words. No offer of comfort came out. He simply held her hands, rubbing his thumb gently over hers. He felt rage, anger, sorrow, compassion, and he hurt in places he hadn't known could hurt.

"I'm glad J.D. and Liam were there for you," he offered quietly.

"Me, too," she said. "Now do you understand why they mean so much to me?"

He nodded. "Completely."

"And that night in your hotel room," she said. "Do you understand that as well?"

Jonah nodded, continuing to stroke her hand. "Have you been with anyone since that… Since you were…"

"Raped?" She smiled ruefully. "You can say the word, it won't kill you. Or me."

"I know," he said and shrugged. "It's just difficult to compartmentalize without wanting to do permanent physical damage to the individuals responsible."

She smiled and it reached her eyes. "That's just your protective instincts going into overdrive. The thing is, Jonah, I had to learn to forgive them, so I could move on with my life. And I thought I had, until I met you." She stopped, stalled and took a long breath. "No… I haven't. That's the answer to your question. I've tried. I've dated. I've allowed myself to feel desire. But something always gets in the way. Fear," she admitted. "Fear of being out of control. Of being suffocated…which is irrational, I know, since the men I've dated have all been very nice and nonthreatening. I've talked to a therapist, and in the end it was clear to me that all I had to do was wait for the right person. That night, with you, that's the closest I've ever been to making love with someone. And yet, I still panicked… I still couldn't go through with it." The oven timer buzzed and she got up, wrapping her arms around herself. When she got to the other side of the counter she looked at him. "Does knowing this about me make you want to run a mile?"

"Not at all."

"Then you're a brave man," she said with a brittle laugh. "The thing is, I want to have a normal life—one that includes sex," she said bluntly.

Jonah stared at her, confused by the intensity of his

own feelings. This was a crossroads for both of them. He could leave before they got too involved, before desire and chemistry turned into something more. Especially now that things were even more complicated.

The thing was, the idea of leaving her, of not seeing her again, made him physically ache inside.

He got to his feet and moved to the other side of the counter. "How about we park this whole…sex thing… and just hang out today."

Her brows rose dramatically. "Just hang out?"

He nodded. "Although I would like a cookie."

She laughed and the sound touched his heart in a way he wasn't used to. All the emotional barriers he'd erected were slowly crumbling because of Connie.

For the first time in his life, Jonah was faced with a startling reality: he was genuinely interested in getting to know a woman and not just circumnavigating the quickest route to her bed. He wanted to spend the day getting to know her. He wanted to know her favorite color. Her favorite food. What movies she enjoyed. What songs made her cry. If she liked rainy days. Or snowball fights. Anything. Everything. He wanted all of her. Which meant he was heading for major heart trouble.

Connie couldn't recall ever having a lovelier day. They stayed indoors for the most part, except for the half an hour they took taking the dogs to the park. She made an early lunch, which they ate in front of the television, and then they played Scrabble for a lazy hour or so, only to discover than Jonah knew way more complicated words than she did. She talked through her plans to renovate the old house room by room and listened to his suggestions about adding a bathroom to the master suite. She baked a little more in the afternoon, and by three they were on the couch and she was resting in the crook of his arm.

"This is nice," she said easily, curling her legs up.

"Want to make out for a while?"

Connie touched his chin and the tiny cleft there. "I thought sex was parked for the day."

He chuckled. "Making out is not sex, Connie. It's—" he ran a hand around her nape and drew her closer "—a kiss. Or two."

His mouth touched hers. "Or three."

True to his word, he didn't touch her below the shoulders. They kissed, gently at first, then slowly with more heat. Connie relaxed and pressed against him, knowing he was half-aroused, but also knowing he would never take more that she was prepared to give. If she had any doubts that she was halfway in love with him, they disappeared that chilly afternoon.

"By the way," he said, twirling a lock of her hair between his fingers. "Mom is expecting you for Thanksgiving this week."

Connie pressed closer. "I'm looking forward to it."

"I'm heading back to Portland in the morning," he reminded her.

She sighed. "I know. Don't forget you have to see you dad before you go. And promise me you won't argue with him."

He didn't make his usual scowling face at the term, which it made her happy inside. "I know and I promise. But I'll be back Wednesday afternoon."

"I guess I'm going to have to get used to this long-distance thing."

He nodded. "For now."

She craned her neck around. "Does that mean you might not always live in Portland?"

He shrugged. "My life is there. My work. My friends," he said and exhaled heavily. "But my mom is here… and you're here…that's quite an incentive to think about moving."

"Kathleen would like that."

He grasped her chin. "What about you?"

"Oh," she teased and drew his mouth closer. "I'm sure I could learn to cope."

He didn't leave until eight o'clock, and he did so with a lingering kiss under the porch light. Connie was desperately unhappy the moment his taillights faded in the distance, but she knew it was wise to let him go home. She'd been tempted to ask him to stay, but it had been an emotional day and she needed time to separate her feelings of gratitude and friendship from her growing sexual desire. And she would.

Making love with Jonah was inevitable. She knew that. She wanted it to happen.

But until then, she had things she needed to do. The hotel was fully booked up until the end of January, and Connie needed to be at her sharpest over the holiday season. Liam looked to her for extra support during the busier times, and she would never want to disappoint him.

She arrived at work early on Monday morning, thinking about Jonah and his meeting with his father, and sent Jonah a supportive text. He responded with a smiley face emoji with a kiss attached, and she was still smiling like a schoolgirl when Liam arrived a little after eight thirty.

"You look happy," he remarked and placed an envelope on her desk. "No doubt that's got something to do with my annoying little brother."

She shrugged and grinned. "Maybe. What's this?" She asked and picked up the envelope. "It's too early for a Christmas bonus."

"Take a look."

Connie opened envelope, scanned the letter inside and then stared at her boss in shock.

"Are you serious?"

"Perfectly."

"Assistant manager? Me?"

Liam nodded. "You deserve it, Connie. I need to step back a bit now that Kayla and Jack are part of my life, and there's no one I trust more with the hotel than you."

Connie looked at the offer letter. More money. Way more. More responsibility. Kudos and reward for her years of loyal service. Tears sprang to her eyes and she managed a shaky smile.

"No tears," Liam warned and held up his hand. "Is that a yes?"

"Can I think about it overnight?"

He frowned for a second. "Of course. And you would also need to find your replacement here. Someone who can put up with me as well as you do."

She thought about how proud she was to have earned the promotion, and how excited she was to share the news with Jonah. Silly, she supposed. She had closer friends, people she'd known longer. But it felt right to tell him her good news.

As for why she wanted to think about it—she wasn't quite sure. But something was holding her back. She shrugged off the feeling and went about her day, looking forward to talking to Jonah.

Jonah's Monday morning meeting with J.D. started exactly as he expected—with enough tension between them to put them both in a bad mood. But he held back his resentment long enough to take a quick tour of the old building and offer his advice.

"The place has been vacant for years," J.D. explained. "But most of the commercial real estate on this side of the river is new and tenanted. This used to be a steel fabrication factory and I'd like to see something here that could be used for manufacturing. It would be good for the town, you know. For employment and the local economy."

"It wouldn't do your bank balance any harm, either," Jonah said as they walked through the ground floor and then back out into the abandoned parking area.

J.D. shrugged. "Real estate is my thing. Just like running the hotel is Liam's thing, or medicine is Kieran's thing and designing buildings is yours. We all have our purpose and our passion."

Jonah wasn't about to disagree. "It's certainly not worth a renovation," he said as he looked around. "Knock it down and build something new."

J.D. nodded. "Would you design it?"

Jonah's back twitched. "I can recommend someone else who lives closer to—"

"I don't want someone else," J.D. said quickly. "I want you."

"Why?"

"You know why. To be a part of something together. To help us heal our relationship."

He stared at his father, ignoring the way his chest constricted. "We don't really have a relationship."

"Yes, we do," J.D. refuted. "A bad one. I want to try to fix that."

"You're trying too hard."

"One of us has to," J.D. said quietly. "Otherwise, we'll keep going around in circles. I don't want that for us, Jonah. I want us to get along. And I want you to have a real relationship with your brothers."

"It doesn't matter what you want," Jonah said, remembering that he'd promised Connie he wouldn't argue with J.D., and the memory of that promise kept him from losing his cool. "And I'll work out my relationship with my brothers in my own way, and my own time."

"And us?"

He sighed heavily. "I'll think about it."

J.D. looked surprised and then smiled. "Okay…great. Maybe we could—"

"One step at a time," Jonah said quickly. "Don't push me. And don't expect too much."

"I can't help it," J.D. admitted. "My children are the most important things in the world to me."

"Is that how you make it right with yourself?" Jonah asked, his chest tightening. "By thinking about how important your kids are to you? If that was really the case, you wouldn't have had an affair with my mother, when you already had a devoted wife, three young kids and another on the way."

J.D. raised his hands. "I made a mistake and I—"

"Yeah," Jonah shot back. "I know. I'm right here."

"I didn't mean that you were the mistake," J.D. said wearily.

"Save it," Jonah snapped and waved a dismissive hand. "I have to go. See you around."

But J.D. clearly wasn't done with him as he followed him to his car. "Please…let's talk about this."

"About what?" Jonah shot back. "About how you were never there? About how I got the leftovers of your real life as a father?"

"I tried to be there when I could," J.D. insisted. "But it was hard. I was…torn."

"Hard?" Jonah echoed the word incredulously. "Seriously? Do you want to know what's hard? Knowing my very existence is your mistake. And knowing there's not a damned thing I can do about it."

Having had more conversation than he wanted, Jonah left then and arrived in Portland a few hours later. He drove straight home from the airport and managed to get some work done before calling it a day around five o'clock. He unpacked his suitcase, threw on a load of laundry, then showered and changed into jeans and a sweatshirt. He searched through the refrigerator for something he could throw together for dinner, and when he found nothing, ordered a pizza. He really did need to work out where he wanted to be, since the constant commuting between Cedar River and Portland was starting to take a toll on his life, both socially and professionally. He couldn't remember the last time he'd gone out for drinks with his friends and he had a couple of work projects that were hovering on the edge of deadlines.

Cedar River was taking over his life. Not just Connie. But J.D. He was sick of listening to the other man tell him how hard it was for him.

I made a mistake…

There it was…in a nutshell.

He called Connie that night and was instantly put at ease when he heard her voice on the other end of the line. She told him about the job offer from Liam, asking his opinion, and he talked her through the pros and cons, and finally she decided she truly was ready to step up and take on the challenge.

"I'm a little overwhelmed," she admitted. "It's more than I expected."

"But what you deserve," he added. "And Liam knows that. Congratulations."

"Thank you," she said breathlessly, and Jonah felt foolish for missing her as much as he did, knowing she was so many miles away. "How did things go with your dad?"

"J.D. was his usual wonderful self," he said wryly, not embellishing too much. He didn't want Connie to be in the middle of his argument with his father. "And I mostly behaved myself, as I promised you I would."

"I'm glad. To be honest," she said, her voice lowering, "I'm a little worried about him."

Jonah's insides contracted. "Why is that?"

She sighed. "I don't know...he just doesn't seem like himself. He hardly spends any time at the hotel these days. I'm not sure what he does with himself."

"I'm sure he's fine," Jonah said, dismissing the uneasiness in his chest.

The conversation set the tempo for the next evening. He called around nine o'clock and they chatted for an hour about nothing in particular. By the time the call was ending, he was torn between happiness and a deep-rooted longing that defied anything he'd ever felt before.

"So, I'll see you tomorrow night?" he inquired, his voice a husky rasp.

"Yes. Absolutely. It's my turn to cook for you."

"Do you have more of those cookies?"

"I made you a special batch," she said and laughed. "And I made some for your mom."

"I can't wait to see you," he admitted.

"Me, too."

"Goodnight, Connie. Sweet dreams."

He ended the call, his head consumed with images of the woman who had somehow invaded his thoughts, and his heart.

By Wednesday evening, Connie was a bag of nerves. She put on her favorite green dress, brushed her hair until it shone and applied a hint of makeup. She knew Jonah liked her freckles, and she wanted them to show. He arrived at six thirty, a bottle of wine in one hand and a bouquet of miniature pink roses in the other. He kissed her forehead and patted the dogs, who had all accepted his appearance as though it was the most normal thing in the world.

Dinner was quiet. They ate, drank some wine and talked about their respective weeks. Connie asked him about his plans for Christmas.

"I was going to spend the holiday with my mom, as usual," he said, watching her over the rim of his glass, and Connie saw the way his eyes darkened. "And you, I hope."

"What about the O'Sullivans?" she asked, fighting the butterflies racing through her belly at the way he watched her. "They'll want to see you."

He shrugged. "Maybe."

"You promised to make an effort, remember?"

"I know," he said and reached across the table to grasp her hand. He ran his middle finger down her palm, and the caress was incredibly erotic. She met his gaze, saw the heat in his eyes and swallowed hard. The mood between them had shifted, going from companionable and friendly to something else…something more.

"Are you going to make love to me?" she asked softly.

Jonah turned her hand over, got to his feet and gently pulled her to stand. "Actually," he said quietly, drawing her close, "I was thinking that maybe you'd like to make love to me."

"Oh," she said and sighed. "Okay."

"Where's your bedroom?"

Connie led him down the hallway and into her bedroom. The lilac coverlet, pale mauve walls and paisley prints had remained unchanged for years, and she spotted a smile on his face as she flicked on the bedside light.

"It's nice," he said and released her. "Very…you."

Connie stood still, knees knocking, her breath shallow. "So, here we are."

He smiled, slipped off his shoes and took his wallet from his khakis. She watched as he extracted a couple of small foil packets and placed them on the bedside table.

Protection. Right. Suddenly the room seemed much smaller.

"This is really happening," she said softly.

"Only if that's what you want," he said and moved around the bed. "If you want to go back into the living room, that's what we'll do."

She shook her head. "No…I want to stay. I want this." She paused, taking a breath. "I want you."

His mouth curved into a smile. He looked so sexy it took her breath away. "Okay…then come here."

She took a step, and then another, until she was in front of him. "I don't know how—"

"Shh," he whispered and grabbed her hands, holding them against his chest. "Undress me."

Connie met his gaze, trembling from head to toe as her fingers traveled up his chest and reached the top button on his shirt. It came undone easily. And then the next. And the next, until she was at the waistband and she pulled the shirt free. His chest was smooth and tanned and perfectly sculpted. She took a moment, remembering how much she wanted him, thinking of his kisses, his touch and how it was exactly what she yearned for. Connie pressed her palms against his skin and moved downward until she reached his belt. He sucked in a sharp breath as her fingers touched his belly, and she smiled.

"Tickles," he said softly, grinning.

Connie undid the belt and slipped it from the loops, tossing it to the floor, and then, with her bravado building, she pushed the shirt off his shoulders and pulled his arms through the sleeves. He really was gorgeous. All lean muscle and sinew, with a trail of hair running from his navel downward. She swallowed hard as her fingers fumbled with the snap on his khakis. She'd never really seen a man completely naked before—only on television and in her dreams of Jonah since their brief night together all those months ago—and being so close to him, inhaling the scent of his cologne, feeling his muscles tense beneath her inexperienced hands, was suddenly a powerful turn-on. She was nervous but not afraid. For the first time in her life, she felt free and whole and knew that being with him was going to be amazing. His arms were at his sides and he didn't move as she touched him.

She took a long breath and then pulled down the zipper. He was hard against her hand, but he still didn't move, didn't make a grab for her and scare her witless. He was in complete control of himself. Connie's entire body shook, and he reached up and grasped her chin, tilting her head toward him.

"You're okay," he assured her gently. "There's no rush."

She nodded. "Help me with the rest."

He grinned and quickly ditched the remainder of his clothes. She drank in the sight of him, and then, when looking wasn't nearly enough, she touched him tentatively, stroking his chest. His arms. His back. And still he didn't move, didn't flinch, didn't take anything from her. He was giving her what she needed. He was giving her trust. And honor. And everything that had been taken from her so long ago.

She went to undo the top button on her dress, but his hand came up and clasped around hers.

"Not yet," he whispered. "Not until you are one hundred percent sure. I want you to feel safe with me," he said. "I want you to know that I will never take anything from you that you are not giving me willingly. That's what making love is, Connie. Or at least, that's what it should be. Two people who trust one another," he said with deliberate emphasis. "But I know that your trust needs to be earned. So *you* touch *me* all you want. And when you're ready to trust me, that's when I'll kiss you. That's when *I'll* touch you."

Tears filled her eyes. "I don't want to disappoint you."

He chuckled and wiped the tears from her eyes with his thumb. "You're so beautiful, Connie. And very sexy. I know you don't really believe that—but it's true. That's what I see when I look at you. And," he said, his voice cracking, "I can never give back what was taken from you. I can never make it right. But here, tonight, there's just you and me. Just two people who have an intense connection and want to be together. You could never disappoint me." He touched her face, cradling her cheek. "Simply being here with you makes me happy."

He dropped his hand and moved toward the bed, sitting up against the headboard, legs stretched out, unmistakably aroused and completely uninhibited. And Connie felt more alive and more powerful than she ever had in her life. She stripped off her dress with a confidence she didn't know she possessed and stood by the bed wearing only her bra and panties. Neither were particularly sexy, but beneath Jonah's visual appraisal, the stretchy black lace made her feel sensual and exotic, but still, her uncertainty lingered.

Connie shook her head. "I don't know what to do."

He grinned. "Whatever you want. You have my permission."

"I'm nervous," she admitted.

"I know. But you're perfectly safe," he insisted softly. "I won't hurt you. You won't hurt me."

He was right. She would never hurt him. And he would never hurt her—Connie knew that deep in her soul. And she understood what he was giving her—his complete surrender.

For Connie, the following hour was like a sensual awakening, a journey of self-discovery she'd never imagined she would take. She touched him, stroked him, ran her trembling fingertips along every angle and sinew. And he allowed her the freedom to take what she wanted…what she needed. She kissed him. She met his lips with her own and felt the erotic slide of his tongue around hers. She roamed over him with her mouth, her tongue, her hands, and in the back of her mind she was waiting for the panic to set in. But it never came. Instead she experienced freedom, as though she was finally throwing off the shackles of that awful day ten years ago. And this man everyone told her was cold and unfriendly and who didn't try to fit in, who didn't care about anyone, had given her the opportunity to grab that freedom. She made him moan, she made him writhe, and he could have easily taken control…but he didn't. He allowed her to take the lead, because he knew it was what she needed to rid herself of her fear and, for the first time in her life, take charge of her sensuality.

"Connie," he said raggedly as she kissed him. "You're killing me."

She knew that. And she loved him for it.

I love this man.

Admitting it to herself strengthened her resolve. And her desire.

And just like that, Connie felt real freedom for the first time in her adult life. Freedom from fear. From anger. From blame. She stripped off her underwear and knelt beside him, grabbing the condom off the bedside table.

"Are you sure?" he asked.

She nodded. "Never surer."

"Tell me what you want," he urged gently. "What you need."

"You," she said simply. "Just you."

"Okay," he said and took the condom, quickly sheathing himself. "But if at any time you want to stop and—"

"Jonah," she said and placed a fingertip against his mouth. "Stop talking."

She rolled and lay back, holding out her hands, feeling powerful and completely in control. She smiled and invited him closer and he obliged immediately, moving over her, his weight resting on his arms.

"Is this okay?" he asked, placing one leg between hers.

Connie nodded and rested her hands on his shoulders. "Perfect."

"You're not…afraid?"

She shook her head. "Not at all."

He kissed her hotly, plunging his tongue into her mouth in an erotic onslaught. She kissed him back, every sense she possessed heightened. He touched her, asking first, whispering his intent as his hand moved along her body, down her rib cage and lower still. Connie waited for the fear to resurface, but none came. She felt only desire and complete and utter surrender to her senses. His touch was gentle, but firm, his caress erotic and achingly tender. He took her up, driving her crazy, making her want him in ways she hadn't imagined possible. And then, once she was at the brink of complete surrender, they were together, joined in the most intimate way possible. There was no discomfort. No pain. No threat. It was breathtaking, joyous, overwhelming. When he moved, she moved. When he kissed her, she kissed him back, matching the slow and seductive rhythm he created that suited them both, and suddenly she was moving her hips in a way that came to her as naturally as breathing. And then she was gone, swept up in a vortex of pleasure so intense it sucked the breath from her lungs. She said his name over and over, felt him meet her in that same place, as release, white-hot and earth-shattering, sent them both over the edge.

When it was over, Connie drew air into her lungs. She didn't move. Her legs were numb, every part of her body suddenly übersensitive. Her breasts ached and she noticed that her nipples were peaked and hard. But she felt good. She felt wonderful.

She met Jonah's gaze. His chest was rising and falling, and he sounded raspy and out of breath as he swung his legs off the bed.

"Where are you going?" she asked, laying on the bed, her hair mussed, her body still craving him.

"Bathroom. Be back in a moment," he promised and left the room.

When he returned, Connie was lying on her side, the sheet draped over herself. As soon as he reached the bed, he tugged the sheet from her.

"You won't be needing that," he said and reached for her. "Are you okay? I didn't hurt you?"

She shook her head. "You didn't hurt me. It was wonderful."

He rolled her over and she took a moment, waiting for the fear and feeling of suffocation to come. But it didn't. She felt only a yearning to feel him inside her again.

"Promise me something," he insisted.

"What?"

"That if anything I do ever makes you feel uncomfortable when we're together like this, you'll tell me."

His consideration and sweetness touched Connie to her very core. "I will," she promised. "But that's not likely, is it, considering what just happened."

"I hope not," he said and kissed her softly. "You feel so good," he said and ran his hand along her hip, dipping gently between her legs.

Connie giggled and searched for his mouth, dragging it down to hers. His hands and fingers wreaked magic. And when he possessed her again, he was in complete command, making her mindless with pleasure, both giving and taking. It was beautiful and soulful, and afterward she cried a little as he held her.

"I don't want this night to end," she admitted later.

"Me, either," he said and tucked her head beneath his chin, cradling her safely in his arms.

They talked for a while, earnest words that she'd kept locked inside herself for so long. Afterward, he held her as though she was the most precious thing in the world.

And then, when she was drifting off to sleep in his embrace, Connie sighed, content and irrevocably in love with him.

Chapter Nine

"You know, you really don't have to bring this much stuff," Jonah said as he watched Connie pack a second basket with food. "There's only going to be the three of us."

She shrugged, looking effortlessly beautiful in a long-sleeved red dress and cowboy boots. Her incredible hair was down, and all he wanted to do was fist a handful of it and drag her mouth to his. He couldn't get enough of the feel of her, the scent of her, the taste of her. They'd made love that morning, but he wanted her again.

"I know," she said and shrugged. "I want the day to be special, that's all."

"It will be," he promised. "Although I should warn you, Mom's matchmaking is going to be in overdrive."

Connie looked pensive. "Are you going to tell her the truth about us?"

"I don't kiss and tell."

"I meant," Connie said and tapped his arm, "are you going to say we're...you know...involved?"

"Connie," he said and grasped her chin and kissed her briefly and soundly. "I think it's pretty obvious to the world that you and I are involved. I won't need to spell it out to my mom. She's going to take one look at me and know that I'm crazy about you."

She smiled. "Are you?"

"Absolutely," he admitted and then promptly changed the subject. "Let's go or we'll be late."

Of course, they weren't going to be late. They were actually early. It was barely two o'clock when they pulled up outside his mother's house. Jonah grabbed the baskets from the back seat and opened the gate, ushering Connie up the path and onto the porch.

"Sweetie," his mother said as she opened the door. "I'm so glad you're here."

"Me, too, Mom," he said and kissed her cheek.

"And it's lovely to have you join us, Connie."

Jonah looked at his mother, saw her cat-that-got-the-cream smile and knew he was totally busted. His mom could read him like a book. "Yes, Mom," he said before the inquisition started as they headed up the hallway and into the kitchen. "Connie and I are here *together*."

"I'm delighted to hear it."

He knew she would be. Jonah began to smile and then noticed there were four place settings on the table. He frowned and looked out the window, spotting a familiar SUV parked at the rear of the house. His suspicions soared and he looked at his mother, thinking that she looked uncharacteristically frazzled.

Jonah placed the baskets on the counter and spoke. "Mom, what's going on?"

"It was all my idea," she said and then turned at a sound coming from the doorway.

J.D.

"You're not serious," he demanded, his irritation rising.

"Perfectly," his mother replied. "I thought it would be a good chance for the two of you to spend some time together."

Jonah didn't dare look at J.D. "We spent time together on Monday," he reminded her, since he'd told her about the meeting during their weekly telephone call.

"That was for an hour," she said and sighed. "I mean some quality time."

"If you'd rather I leave," J.D. said quietly, "then I—"

"Am I talking to you?" Jonah said, his anger gaining momentum.

He felt Connie's hand on his wrist, squeezing hard. "It'll be okay," she assured him and nodded, then whispered. "Just try. Please."

But he didn't want to try. He didn't want J.D. encroaching on his life, his mother or Connie. But he didn't want a scene, either. Not in front of Connie. "Sure," he shrugged. "Whatever."

He sat at the table and watched as the two most important women in his life unpacked the baskets and began chatting about food and Thanksgiving and how he and Connie had spent an hour visiting the veterans' home earlier that morning, distributing the cookies she'd baked for the residents.

And J.D. stood on the sidelines, watching, saying nothing. Exactly how it should be.

"This looks amazing, Connie," his mother said. "I can't thank you enough."

Jonah didn't miss the edge in her words. Kathleen had been itching for him to get a girlfriend for ages, but

Jonah's previous relationships had been fleeting at best. But Connie was different—and he sensed his mother knew as much.

Jonah sat on his temper and endured a torturous hour of cocktails and chitchat, pretending that he was fine with sharing a family occasion with J.D. Because he wasn't fine. Far from it.

"Why aren't you at Liam's today?" he asked when they had all taken their seats at the table and the meal was served. He knew why, since Liam had mentioned the fact at Kieran's wedding, but he wanted to hear it directly from J.D.

J.D. shifted in his chair. "Gwen is there. I didn't want to make this difficult for her."

"No, just for us," Jonah muttered harshly.

"I asked your father to join us today," his mother added.

Jonah felt Connie's fingers digging into his thigh. "Why?" He shrugged. "Oh, yeah. So we can bond."

"Would that be so terrible?" Kathleen asked.

The tension around the table was palpable, but Jonah wasn't about to back down. It didn't matter that his mother had asked him to come. As far as he was concerned, J.D. was intruding on his family. "I don't know what you think is going to happen here. But it's not going to end in all of us being some happy family."

"We could at least find some common ground," J.D. said quietly. "If you'd stop behaving like a spoiled child."

Jonah sprang to his feet and pushed the chair back. "I will when you stop behaving as though you have some right to be here."

J.D. stood. "I do have the right. I'm your father."

Jonah tossed his napkin onto his half-empty plate. "You're nothing to me. I'm a *mistake*, remember?"

He walked from the room, so wound up he could barely draw air into his lungs. It was not how he'd imagined the day would go. He'd thought it would be a relaxing, happy afternoon with the two most important women in his life. That he'd take Connie home and make love to her. Not this. Not J.D. continuing to insinuate himself into his life at every turn.

He was by the window when he heard his name. Connie stood in the doorway, her arms crossed. He didn't need to meet her gaze to know he was in for a lecture.

"What are you doing?"

"Letting off steam."

"Is this really how you want things to play out with your father today?"

He met her stare. "Stop calling him that."

"You can't deny the truth, Jonah. Can't you at least try, for your mom's sake?"

"What does my mother have to do with it?" he demanded.

Connie's expression softened. "Surely you can see what I see."

He didn't like what she was suggesting. That after so many years, his mother might still… He couldn't even bear the thought. And yet, he understood. And it increased his anger tenfold. "That's impossible. Not after all this time."

Connie shrugged. "It's obvious they care about one another. I also see a woman who is desperately trying to bring you and your dad back together. She clearly has a great capacity for love and doesn't know how to get you to—"

"Spare me the lecture about my mother," he said irritably and moved around the room, looking at things that were both familiar and new. "I think I know her a little better than you do."

"Are you sure? If you'd get out of the way of your own ego for a moment, you'd see that it hurts her every time you turn away from J.D."

"My ego?" he echoed incredulously. "Is that how it's going to be? We're going to get into an argument over J.D.? You're taking his side?"

"I'm on your side," she said quickly. "But you're not thinking about this straight. He's not a bad person. And he desperately wants to be a part of your life. You're so angry at him, you don't know how lucky you really are. I'd give anything to have parents who care about me as much as yours care about you. I haven't seen my parents for three years and they can barely spare the time to send me a birthday card. And after I was assaulted, they came back even less, probably scared that the incident might somehow taint their academic reputation."

Guilt hit him between the shoulders, and he was about to consider her argument when he knocked one of the easels with his shoulder and the cover slipped off. Jonah stared at the painting, recognizing his mother's work immediately. He also recognized the subject.

It was J.D.

He swore loudly and recoiled a little when Connie winced. But it was too much. The picture was new, a work in progress, and J.D. looked as he did now. And something else. Jonah was no art buff, but he saw the emotion in the strokes. The feeling. The love.

He felt sick.

It took about ten seconds for J.D. to enter the room, and Jonah glared at the older man, his rage gathering momentum with every breath. J.D. looked at him and Jonah knew what he was seeing in the portrait was real.

"We wanted to tell you," J.D. said rawly. "We just didn't know how."

He saw his mother move up behind J.D. and place a hand on his shoulder, and Jonah experienced an acute sense of betrayal. And Connie *wasn't* beside him. She was neutral. It made him as mad as hell all over again. He looked at his mother and she nodded.

"Are you out of your mind, Mom?"

"Don't talk to your mother like that," J.D. said.

Jonah clenched his fists, holding on to his temper. "You don't get to tell me what to do," he snapped. "You gave up that right the moment my mother left this town to save your ass thirty years ago!"

J.D. recoiled and stepped back, shaking Kathleen's hand from his shoulder. "We did what we thought was best."

"We?" Jonah shot back. *"You* had nothing to do with it. *My* mom did what was best, for me, for you, for everyone but herself. And growing up I had to stand by and watch her, knowing she missed her family, knowing she'd given everything up to make sure no one else got hurt because of your selfishness. I hate you for doing that. So much."

"I know," J.D. replied. "But I *love* you, and there's not a damned thing you can do about it."

It wasn't what he wanted to hear, and the words simply fueled his rage. "Why can't you leave us alone?" he said, suddenly pounding his fist on the wall.

"Jonah!"

Connie's voice, pulling him back to the land of civility and good sense, to that place where anger and rage couldn't hold him hostage. He turned and saw Connie staring at him incredulously, shaking her head, looking shocked and utterly disappointed.

J.D. spoke again. "Because I love you both too much.

I always have. And one day, if you have a child with the woman you love more than life itself, you'll understand why I could never leave you. You're a part of me," J.D. said, and Jonah saw tears in the other man's eyes. "Whatever you think, you need to know that you were never some terrible secret I wanted to hide from the world." J.D. brushed the wetness from his face. "You're my son. My flesh and blood, just like Liam and Kieran and Sean. And if you have to hate me, then hate me. But don't ever disrespect your mother again."

Jonah's throat burned and he swallowed hard. All he wanted to do was grab Connie and leave, putting as much space between himself and J.D. as possible. He met her gaze and tried to make a connection—but she was staring at him blankly.

Please don't bail on me.

I need you.

"Jonah?"

His mother's voice.

"Yes, Mom."

"Try to understand," she implored. "Your dad and I…we have history. And a long time ago, we loved each other very much. Please don't be mad at me for wanting to feel that again."

"I don't. But he hurt you, Mom. Over and over. He was never there."

"He was there," she said and came up beside J.D. "He was always in my heart."

Jonah shook his head, suddenly spent. "I love you, Mom, but I think you'd be a fool to trust him again." He turned toward Connie. "Let's go."

He ignored J.D., kissed his mother on the cheek and walked down the hallway, lingering on the porch for a moment, waiting for Connie to catch up. When she reached the door she remained beneath the threshold.

"You should go home and cool off," she said quietly.

His gaze narrowed instantly. He knew what that meant. "You're staying?"

She nodded. "I need to help your mom clean up and—"

"*I* need you," he implored.

She shook her head. "No, you don't. You're too busy hating your father to need anything else."

Jonah ran a hand through his hair. "Okay…I lost my cool. Forget about it. I'll be fine."

"I don't doubt it," she said quietly. "It's not you I'm concerned about. It's your mom and J.D."

"You're choosing him over me?"

She made an impatient sound. "I'm choosing to be where I can be the most help."

Jonah was so mad he couldn't think straight. "There's that blind loyalty again. I suppose it's to be expected, since you got your big promotion."

Her eyes glistened. "You're such a jerk."

"And you're as gullible as my mom."

"I guess I'd have to be to get involved with you."

It was a direct hit. And a good one. Jonah took the steps two at a time and headed off to his car. To hell with them. To hell with everybody.

He just wanted to be left alone.

By the time Connie walked back in the kitchen, Kathleen was washing dishes and J.D. was wrapping bowls in plastic wrap. It looked like a cozy domestic scene, except for the palpable undercurrent of hurt in the room.

"He's gone," she said and rested a hand on the counter.

Kathleen smiled brittlely. "You stayed. He'll take that personally."

She shrugged. "He's a big boy—he'll get over it."

"Probably. Once he's finished brooding."

Connie laughed. "Yeah."

"You love him," Kathleen said quietly. "Don't you?"

She thought about denying it but shrugged instead. "Yes, I do. Although right at this moment, I'm not sure why."

"Because he's honest and strong and caring. He gets that from his father."

"Don't tell him that," J.D. quipped and grinned. "Kid hates my guts."

"I don't think he does," Connie said gently. "He's trying to, I admit. But he's not good at hate—that's why he's so torn up about it."

J.D. nodded. "It kills me to see him hurting."

"Me, too," Connie admitted. "But sometimes you have to leave the wounded bear alone."

J.D. pressed a hand to his belly and frowned. "Maybe."

"Ulcer acting up?" she asked.

He nodded. "Probably. But don't worry... I'll be fine."

Connie wasn't so sure. There was a gray pallor to J.D.'s complexion. "I can go and get your medication if you—"

J.D. interrupted her by coming around the counter and hauling her into a bear hug. "You're a sweet girl, Connie. Don't let Jonah upset you... Underneath his grumbling he's got a good heart."

"I know," she said and squeezed her eyes tightly shut. "It's why I love him."

"Then go to him," J.D. urged and pulled keys from his pocket. "Take my car. We'll be fine."

Connie nodded, and a few minutes later she was driving to Jonah's apartment. But he wasn't at home. She tried the hotel and even JoJo's, but nothing. It was over an hour before she headed home and was stunned to discover Jonah's car outside her house.

He was on the porch. Connie unlocked the gate and headed up the path, her feet heavy, her insides aching. He looked so unhappy, so raw and vulnerable, that every ounce of love she possessed rose up and expanded her heart. But she was mad at him, too.

She rattled the keys in her hand. "The gate was locked. Did you jump the fence?"

"Yes."

She sighed. "Why are you here?"

"To apologize."

"It's not me who needs an apology."

He threaded his fingers through his hair and got to his feet. "I'll speak to my mom later."

"I meant J.D."

"I'm not—"

"He's the one you argued with. Again," she added. "And I think you put a dent in your mom's wall."

Her words hung in the air, but they had to be said. His actions had consequences.

"I didn't mean to upset you. I blew a fuse. I'm sorry."

It was a meager offering. And not enough. "You need to say that to him."

She walked up the steps and opened the door, desperate to touch him, to feel his arms around her, to help heal his hurt and soothe the pain in his heart. But…he needed to take responsibility first.

His hand came out and he grasped her wrist, holding her steady. "Don't do that. Don't choose him over me."

Connie's insides lurched. "I'm not. I'm choosing what's right."

He released her immediately. "He intruded today."

She shook her head. "No, he didn't. You heard your mom—they're in love."

"Don't say that."

"It's the truth and you need to accept it. Otherwise your mother will be forced to make a choice…and you don't want that…not really." Connie sighed heavily. "Are you coming inside?"

"No," he said stubbornly.

"Then why are you here?" she demanded.

"I wanted to make sure you were okay." He looked to the road. "I see you borrowed J.D.'s rig."

"He was concerned about you," she said gently. "I went to your apartment and the hotel. I didn't expect to find you here."

He ran a weary hand through his hair and scowled. "This is about the only place that feels like home to me in this damned town."

Connie's belly lurched and she was lost. As angry and filled with rage as he was…as irrational as he was when it came to his father, Connie was unable to turn him away. "Then come inside."

"If I do, then I'll want to make love to you. And that's probably the last thing on your mind at the moment."

Not the last thing. Because as annoyed as she was with his behavior, she wanted him. She wanted the heat and sweat and pleasure she knew he could bestow. And she wanted his possession. She wanted him over her, around her, inside her. She wanted to find sweet oblivion in the hard angles of his body. She wanted his mouth on hers, his hand between her legs, his hips meshed with hers.

"Then let's do that," she suggested. "Let's make love. Let me help you forget all the anger and the hurt that you have in your heart."

His eyes glittered. "I can't help how I feel."

"Yes," she assured him. "You can. Please try."

He took a moment, staring at her, then he swallowed hard. "Okay... I will, for you."

Connie shook her head a fraction. "Not for me. For yourself."

He moved, hauling her into his arms, his mouth crashing down on hers passionately. The baskets landed at her feet and Jonah walked her backward until they were in the hallway and the door was locked. They made it to her bedroom and clothes were peeled off. He nudged her thighs apart, touching her, finding her wet and ready, their mouths fused, their breathing the only sound in the room. He hovered over her, looking into her face, and Connie felt a connection so acute it almost stilled her heart. She wound her arms around him, settling on his hips and urging him closer, realizing that all her fear of sexual intimacy had disappeared. Even like this—when their tempers were on high alert and they were in the midst of an argument—their passion, their longing for one another, overrode anything else.

He moved. She complied. He urged. She answered. It went on and on, with Jonah remaining over her, supporting his weight on his strong arms, eyes open, the pace he created driving them both toward an erotic ride. Connie felt the pleasure rise and she let go, moaning his name, feeling him shudder above her, and then he collapsed, heat emanating from every pore, his breath a ragged testimony to the intensity of his release. She felt powerful. Like a goddess, holding him gently in her arms in his most vulnerable moment.

He moved, rolled and then flopped beside her, one arm flung over his face.

And then he swore. Loudly. A curse word she hadn't heard him say before.

"What?"

He groaned. "We didn't use protection."

Right. An obvious and glaring omission. She patted his arm reassuringly and mentally calculated her cycle. "It'll be okay. I'm sure nothing will happen."

He rolled and lay on his side, admiring her in a way only he could, his hand suddenly flat on her belly. "If you get pregnant, we get married."

Married?

"Is that a proposal?" she teased, even though she was aching inside, and then changed her tone when she felt him go rigid beside her. "I'm kidding. Don't stress."

"I'm perfectly serious," he said, splaying his palm deliberately and possessively over her stomach. "I'm not going to bring an illegitimate child into the world."

"I don't think legitimacy matters so much these days."

"It does to me," he said firmly, continuing to palm her belly. "I'd want to do it right. I'd marry you," he assured her. "And I would be faithful."

Connie's heart constricted. "I know. But it's probably not an issue."

"You'd tell me, wouldn't you, if you were pregnant?"

She rolled and faced him. "Of course."

He relaxed a little. "I'm sorry. I've never been that careless. But you…" He sighed heavily. "You make me forget things."

"Sometimes," she said gently and grabbed his hand, holding it against her breast, "sometimes you have to forget things. And forgive. I've had to… If I didn't, then making love with you wouldn't feel like this for me. I'd be trapped beneath those bleachers forever. But meeting you changed things for me…it made me believe I could make love with someone and not feel anxious or afraid. I've had to let go of anger, Jonah. And so do you."

"I can't," he admitted.

"You have to," she insisted. "You say you want to be a better man than he is. Then be better. Be stronger. And forgive him."

"You're asking for too much."

"I'm asking for everything," she corrected. "Forgiveness is the key."

"I thought that was love?" he said, his eyes never bluer, his gaze never more intense.

"First you forgive," she said and traced a fingertip down his chest. "And then you love."

As he kissed her, as they made love again and she came apart in his arms, Connie hoped she'd managed to get through his thick hide. Because if she didn't, she suspected they were doomed.

Chapter Ten

The following Friday, Jonah was at work, in a meeting with one of the firm's top clients, when he got a call from his mother. He let the call ring out and when the meeting was over checked his messages. His mother's voice, saying that J.D. was moving into her house, made him feel as though someone had slapped him across the face.

He called Connie, but the call went to voice mail. He'd hardly spoken to her since Thanksgiving, citing work and meetings and any other excuse he could think of to avoid hearing the disappointment and censure in her voice. And he hadn't committed to returning to Cedar River anytime soon. He'd left early Friday morning, changing his flight, both happy and miserable to be leaving town, and her. But he felt suffocated by everything that had happened. Because he knew what she thought—that he should forgive J.D. and race toward the O'Sullivans with open arms.

But that wasn't who he was.

All his life he'd kept himself from feeling anything other than resentment. Self-preservation at its finest. And the only thing that kept him from crying himself to sleep at night when he was a child. J.D.'s part-time father routine got old once Jonah realized it was all he would ever have. He got the scraps, the leftovers of his father's *real* life.

And it hurt.

So, instead of begging for more time and attention, instead of demanding his father share himself equally, Jonah made rage and resentment his ally. And it wasn't long before he'd learned to blame J. D. O'Sullivan for everything and abhor every lying, deceitful thing the other man stood for. His mother tried to make up for J.D.'s long absences in his life, but it never fully healed the feelings of abandonment and rejection.

What he hadn't bargained on was the rest of the O'Sullivans discovering his existence and then wanting to meet him, to bring him into their lives. He still didn't understand it. He was a walking, talking reminder of J.D.'s adultery... He was the result of betrayal and dishonesty. And it still felt like a weight bearing down on his shoulders, even though the O'Sullivans had been mostly pleasant and welcoming. Because it couldn't last. For the moment it was a novelty. *He* was a novelty. He was just waiting for them to tell him he was an intruder, an interloper...a mistake. This fleeting sense of belonging that he'd always secretly hoped for was false. It was inevitable. He knew that. He felt it deep within his bones. Because things in Cedar River were simply too complicated.

He also hadn't bargained on falling for Connie Bedford.

Because he *was* falling. Jonah knew there was more between them than friendship. More than simply great sex. He'd had great sex before. But his connection to Connie was different. Making love to her wasn't just about physical release. Getting her into bed hadn't exorcised his desire for her. It had only amplified it. He wanted her more every time they were together.

He hated feeling vulnerable.

But he still wanted to go back for more.

He stood by the window in his office, looking at the rain beating down on the glass, his head pounding so much he couldn't focus. A month ago nothing had seemed so complicated. He and Connie weren't lovers. He was able to function at work without getting a migraine. And his mother and J.D. weren't shacking up together.

Thinking of his mother brought back the entire scene at Thanksgiving, and once again, he felt guilt and shame bite him between the shoulder blades. Christmas was a few weeks away and he figured he needed to make peace with his mother. She loved the holidays more than anyone he knew, and he didn't want to ruin them for her.

Emotions churning within him, he finally called it a day at three o'clock, managing to book a flight to Rapid City and telling his partners he was taking a couple of days off to sort out some family stuff. He had plenty of time saved up and no one blinked an eye at his decision. He went home, packed a bag and headed for the airport.

He collected a rental car and was back in Cedar River by ten on Friday night. His apartment at the Victorian felt more familiar than he'd expected, more so than his Portland condo. And then he thought about Connie's warm and welcoming home, and her even warmer bed, and he had to fight the urge to call her, knowing it was too late and not wanting to wake her. But he dreamed of her. Long, torturous dreams that made him feel lethargic and weary with wanting for her when he finally dragged himself out of bed the following morning.

He called her at nine o'clock on Saturday morning and it went to voice mail again. He turned up at her house at ten and tapped on the door. She wasn't home, so he called and left a message on her phone. Then he drove to the hotel to see if Connie was working. He headed upstairs and found her at her desk, dressed in her corporate uniform, her hair in a neat topknot. He hovered by the door, watching her as she worked, thinking about how much he'd missed her and realizing it was the first time he'd ever really allowed himself to miss anyone. He ached to touch her, to kiss her, to feel her move beneath him.

"Jonah?" She said his name and was on her feet in a second. "I didn't expect you this weekend."

He shrugged and came into the office. "You're working on a Saturday?"

She smiled and moved closer. "I've been interviewing the last couple of days. Looking for my replacement."

"No easy feat, I'm sure."

"There are a couple of good candidates," she said extra cheerfully. "It's good to see you."

He raised a brow. "Is it? I called you twice."

"I know," she admitted and grabbed her cell phone, ignoring him for a few seconds as she pressed a few buttons. "You didn't leave a message."

He shrugged, annoyed with her for being so blasé. "I didn't realize I had to."

"You said you had a lot of work to catch up on," she said and leaned on the edge of the desk.

"I did. I do. Actually, I'm not sure why I came."

She looked at him. "A booty call?"

"I told you weeks ago," he said irritably. "If I just wanted to get laid, I'd stay in Portland."

Her cheeks blotched with color. "God, you're such an ass sometimes."

He shrugged again. "You're the one ignoring my calls."

"You don't always get to have things your own way," she said and shifted a few files on her desk.

"Ain't that the truth," he said cynically. "I guess you know that J.D. and my mother are planning on moving in together?"

She nodded. "Liam told me."

He made a scoffing sound. "I bet that went over like a lead balloon."

"Actually, he was less surprised by the idea than I thought he would be."

"Maybe he's mellowing due to his sudden domestic bliss," Jonah said mockingly.

"Or maybe he knows that you can't tell someone else how to live their life."

It was a direct dig. "I don't care what J.D. does. I just don't want him doing anything with my mother."

"Too late," she replied. "They're a couple. And happy about it, by the look of things. I went to dinner with them the other night at JoJo's. We talked about you a lot. It's a wonder your ears weren't burning."

Jonah glared at her, very aware that she was making fun of him. She looked so damned beautiful. He stared at her mouth, thinking it looked fuller than he remembered. And her cheeks were tinged with color. And her gray eyes were smoky and sexy and watched him with a kind of sultry awareness. She looked different somehow, and his suspicions rose.

"Are you pregnant?"

She laughed softly. "Is that why you've been weird this week? Because you think I might be pregnant?"

"I haven't been weird," he said. "And you haven't answered the question."

"It's obviously too early to tell," she said quietly. "And not likely, in any case."

Jonah experienced an odd disappointment. Maybe she looked different because he'd been hoping that she *was* pregnant and because he was looking for any excuse to keep seeing her. He shrugged as casually as he could manage. "Fair enough."

Her mouth thinned. "You look tired."

"It's been a long week," he said, wanting to kiss her senseless. He changed the subject. "Would you come to Portland next weekend for a visit? I'd like to show you my city. I could get you an airplane ticket and pick you up at the—"

"Are you going to make peace with J.D.?" she asked bluntly.

Jonah rocked back a little on his heels. Their conversation always seems to navigate back to J.D. "I hadn't planned on it."

"Then…no."

Annoyance spiked his blood. "Are we back to the emotional-blackmail thing again?"

She got to her feet. "It's not that. But your mother and J.D. are happy together. *They're in love.* And sticking your head in the sand isn't going to change that. If you don't learn to accept it, someone is going to get hurt…and I'm afraid that someone will be you. I don't want that for you." She took a heavy breath. "I want you to have the family I know, in your heart, that you want. Which includes your father and your brothers. Nothing can change what J.D. did all those years ago, Jonah, or the choices he made. And I know that you and your mom have been a tight unit for a long time...but things change. People change. People fall in love."

"So, they're in love," he said and laughed humorlessly. "It won't last. He wants my mother because he hasn't been able to have her for the past thirty years. Once he's got her, he'll move on to someone else."

"You don't know that," she shot back. "Your father isn't some serial womanizer. He had an affair...once."

"I don't need reminding...since I'm the product of that fling."

"I think you do need reminding. Although I'm not sure how much good it will do, since you seem determined to see the worst in people, particularly J.D. and Liam," she said, chest heaving. "And in doing so, you'll deny yourself the chance to have a real relationship with two amazing people. What are you so afraid of, Jonah? Inclusion?" she queried. "Or rejection?"

She was so close to working him out, he wanted to bail. No one had ever challenged his beliefs until Connie. Because he'd never allowed himself to get close enough to anyone before. But she was close. Too close. And if he hung around, Jonah knew she would break down his defenses.

"I'd like to know the answer to that one."

J.D.

Jonah glanced toward the door and saw his father. He looked tired. Old.

"What do you want?" he demanded.

"To talk to you," J.D. said quietly.

Jonah frowned. "How did you know I was here?"

"I texted your dad when you arrived," Connie said flatly. "He was downstairs having coffee with Liam and your mother."

Jonah's chest tightened. His mother was at the hotel.

Connie was acting as though *he* was the villain. *She's chosen her side.* His life was imploding. He hurt all over. "I'm leaving."

"Not until we've talked," J.D. said. "I'm concerned about your mother. You've hardly spoken to her this week."

"I've hardly spoken to anyone this week," he shot back, his words directed toward Connie. They'd hardly talked at all, and he'd missed her. That's why he'd bailed from Portland and caught the first flight he could. "I've been working. And I don't need to explain myself to you."

"That's true," J.D. said. "You're a grown man and entitled to live your own life. But it goes both ways," he reminded him.

"Everything all right here?"

It was Liam in the doorway, and Jonah experienced an acute sense of suffocation. He was on one side, they were on the other. And Connie was clearly allied with the O'Sullivans. She was loyal to them, after all. They'd saved her life. She felt indebted to them. She would always choose them. An all-too-familiar ache pierced his heart.

"Everything's fine," J.D. said and nodded.

"Dad, I don't think you should—"

"It's okay," J.D. interrupted Liam with a wave of his hand. "I need to say something to your brother, something that is long overdue. You know, Jonah, you've given me a lot to think about this past week…made me ask myself what I could have done better when it came to being a father to you. And, sure, I could have done everything better. I could have seen you more, talked to you more, explained the situation to you better. But I didn't," J.D. said wearily. "I took the easy route. The coward's way. Because I didn't want to lose you and your mother, but I didn't want to lose Gwen and my family, either. I was selfish and self-important. So, there, I've said it. Everything was my fault. I failed to be a father to you. I let you down. I let your mom down. I let my wife down. And I let Liam and Kieran and Liz and Sean down. I screwed up and left you to pay the price for my failures. I'm sorry, Jonah. And I would like to ask for your forgiveness. Even if you never want to speak to me again."

Jonah stared at J.D., noticing the other man looked unusually red in the face. He looked at Connie and saw she had furrow lines between her brows. And he glanced toward Liam, who had clearly gone into protective mode. Jonah had heard enough, more than he wanted.

"It's too late for absolution," he said.

"Maybe," J.D. replied and ran a hand over his jaw. "But I'm asking anyway."

Jonah's throat tightened. "No."

J.D.'s expression openly crumpled, and Jonah ignored the continuing twitch in his chest. He didn't want to have any reaction. Reaction meant feelings. And feelings were out of the question. He didn't want to have any feelings for J.D. other than the rage and resentment that kept him from falling apart at the seams.

"Okay," the older man said and sighed. "You win. I'm done. I'll end my relationship with your mother and I won't bother you anymore. I'll give you exactly what you want, son. I'll leave you alone."

J.D. turned, and as he walked away, Liam patted his shoulder assuredly. Jonah didn't care. Once the older man was out of sight, Connie muttered something about making sure he was okay and followed him out the office. And then Liam spoke.

"Did you have to do that?" he demanded.

"Do what?" he shot back, his spine straightening.

"Break him."

"I don't know—"

"God, you're a selfish bastard," Liam said roughly. "Do you know how hard it was for him to admit to all that stuff? You don't give an inch, do you? Talking to you is like banging your head against a brick wall. With your holier-than-thou attitude, we might be led to believe that you've never made a single mistake in your life. I knew you were an unforgiving, narrow-minded jerk from the first time we met. I wanted to keep the family away from you because wherever you go, misery seems to follow. But Dad insisted… He said he needed to have you in his life. But you don't make things easy for anyone. *My way or the highway*… There's no middle road with you, no compromise."

The words stung, but Jonah refused to cave. "Are you finished?"

Liam jutted his chin out. "Why, do you want to take a shot at me?"

Jonah's blood curdled. "I'm not going to fight you."

"Smart decision. Even though a good walloping might do you good."

His fists curled and he took a deep breath. Jonah had never been in a fistfight, but if his brother wanted to go a round or two, he'd certainly oblige. Maybe it would help exorcise the demons and rage pressing down on his shoulders. They were close, barely a few feet apart, close enough for one of them to take a swing. Liam looked furious, and his expression fueled Jonah's resentment.

"If you guys start fighting," Connie said from behind them, "two things are going to happen."

Jonah snapped his head around. She was in the doorway, arms crossed, clearly unhappy by the scene they were having. Jonah's gaze connected with hers, and she sighed heavily.

"Where's Dad?" Liam asked.

"Resting in his room," she replied and moved around them, standing point like a referee. "First," she said and looked at Liam, "I'll quit, and you'll have to finish the interviews yourself. And second," she said, staring at Jonah, meeting his gaze with unwavering strength, "I won't see you anymore."

Several seconds of curdling tension passed in silence. And then Liam laughed, the sound so annoying Jonah suddenly did want to punch him in the nose.

"Well," his brother said and stepped back. "I don't think either of us wants to risk that."

"Good," she said and picked up a folder from the desk. "I thought it might be a good time to go over the plans for the museum extension. Only," she added pointedly, "I think we should postpone that idea for another day. I don't think I can trust that either of you can be civil enough to sit in the same room together and not throw a punch."

"I'm good with that," Liam said and raised a hand as he walked toward his office. "I wouldn't want to risk your wrath, Connie. Although you have my word I won't touch a hair on his pretty head."

Once his brother was out of sight, Jonah spoke. "He's such a jerk."

"He was only protecting J.D. That's what people do when they care about someone." She sighed heavily. "We really need to talk."

He nodded. "Would you like to come to my place for dinner?"

"No," she replied, and his heart sank a little. "I'll cook. There's a key under the blue flowerpot on my porch. I'll be here for about another hour. Make yourself at home and I'll see you when I get there."

Jonah nodded, made a half-move toward her and then

changed his mind. He wanted to kiss her. But it wasn't the time or place.

Half an hour later, he was driving toward Connie's. He picked up flowers and doughnuts on the way and made himself at home when he arrived at her house. The scent of baking and flowers haunted him as he moved from room to room, the dogs not far from his heels.

It was close to lunchtime when he started getting antsy. He went to grab his cell from his pocket and realized he must have left it in the car. He was about to walk outside when he saw Connie coming up the path. Grabbing the flowers, he waited for her to come in, noticing that the dogs were unusually subdued when she crossed the threshold. Her hair was out of its ponytail and she dropped her bag in the hallway when she spotted him hovering by the living room door, holding the flowers in his hand.

"A peace offering," he said quietly and smiled. "Sorry for being a jerk before."

Her mouth creased uneasily, and he noticed how crumpled her clothes were, and that she looked far from her usual picture-perfect professional image.

He met her gaze and she spoke, her voice a bare whisper. "Jonah."

"What's wrong?"

"I've been trying to call you."

He took a step forward and explained about his phone being in the car and then dropped the flowers onto the hall table. "What is it?"

She swallowed hard, her eyes glittering. "It's J.D. He collapsed at the hotel. He's in the hospital."

Jonah felt as though a freight train had come to a screeching halt in his head. "What happened?"

She shrugged. "I'm not sure. But we need to go."

"I...I don't..."

"We need to go, Jonah. *Now.*"

He looked at her, felt the raw emotion and tension in her movements, her words, even her ragged breath. And he knew it was bad. His head pounded. His chest ached. And blame settled squarely into his very soul.

What if I killed my father?

Connie drove to the hospital. Not because she thought Jonah incapable of handling a vehicle. But because she needed something to do, something to keep her thoughts away from the image of J.D. sprawled out on the floor in the hotel foyer, pale and gasping for breath. Thankfully the concierge knew CPR and had quickly called 911. But Connie was worried. J.D. was in trouble.

Liam had already left the office and Connie had had to make the terrible phone call. Of course he took control, telling her not to worry, that he would contact his family, and then he'd asked her to call Jonah. But it wasn't the kind of thing to be said over the phone. Face-to-face was best.

But Jonah looked cold. Unmoved. Almost robotic. There was no anger, no resistance, no emotion. Just blankness. Of course, it could be shock, she thought as she tried to talk to him on the way to the hospital and got little response.

By the time they arrived at the ER, almost the whole family was there, including both Gwen and Kathleen, sitting at opposite ends of the waiting room. Connie went to grasp Jonah's hand, but he pulled away, staying on the fringes of the group, hovering in the doorway. She crossed her arms, ignoring the hurt seeping into her bones and trying not to cry, and walked toward Gwen. She sat down, took a long breath and waited.

At least ten minutes passed in uncomfortable silence before Kieran arrived, pale and clearly concerned. "They're doing tests now to determine the severity of the attack. It looks like a combination of his ulcer and his heart."

"He had a heart attack?" Liam asked the obvious question.

Kieran nodded fractionally and sighed. "They're doing an echocardiogram right now to assess the damage."

"Shouldn't you be in there?" Liam shot back.

"I'm a little conflicted here," Kieran replied. "Too close to the patient. He's in good hands with Dr. Parker."

Connie knew Lucy Parker, formerly Lucy Monero. She was a wonderful doctor. She could see how helpless Kieran looked, but knew he was doing the right thing by stepping back. Connie glanced toward Jonah, still standing by the door, arms crossed, his handsome face expressionless. She wanted to shake him and hug him simultaneously.

He met her gaze, and she managed a reassuring smile. But…nothing. He barely blinked. But she spotted the pulse in his neck and saw it was throbbing madly.

No one said anything.

Until Kathleen Rickard spoke.

"Are you happy now?"

Half a dozen sets of eyes zoomed in on Jonah. Connie watched as he straightened and looked at his mother. Kathleen had tears in her eyes, but her chin was held high.

"Mom, I—"

"You've spent so long hating him for what he didn't do," Kathleen said and shook her head. "You didn't bother to spare a thought for whatever he *did* do. I love you, Jonah…but right now, I'm just so angry I can't even look at you."

The sudden silence was deafening.

She felt the blame in the room, the agreement, the combined censure from a group of people who all cared about one another deeply and were silently searching for someone to pin their fears on.

Jonah.

In that moment, he became the outsider he'd always feared.

Connie looked at him, watched as he closed down, and she experienced an acute sense of helplessness. He needed her support. Her backing. But so did the O'Sullivans. And suddenly she was torn—caught between love and loyalty. Worse, she knew that Jonah saw the conflict in her eyes.

He turned and walked out.

Once he was gone, the dynamic in the room changed instantly. She looked around. Everyone started talking. They all relaxed. It saddened Connie to the core of her being. She met Kathleen's gaze and knew the older woman regretted her words. Connie nodded gently and started after Jonah. She had to do something.

Loyalty or love?

In that moment, she chose love.

Chapter Eleven

Jonah sat in the hospital cafeteria and sipped stale coffee he could barely taste. He thought about his life. His choices. Everything he'd said and done to get to where he was.

In his professional life, he was respected and revered and at the top of his field. He had money, friends and a luxurious condo. Women had never been hard to find. Sex had always been casual and meaningless. Shallow experiences that shaped a shallow life. He'd spent his childhood longing for the perfect family, the traditional image of a mom and dad, maybe a sibling or two. What he got was an overprotective mother and a mostly absent father who favored his real family in another state.

What he'd wanted…what he'd needed…was more than he got from J.D.

It had left a hole inside him. A gap that couldn't be filled with success or money or empty sex. So instead, he filled that gap with rage and resentment. And rage and resentment, he'd discovered, were a good shield against feeling *anything* too much. None of his friends noticed. Nor did the women who casually shared his bed. He kept it buttoned up, away from his day-to-day life. But beneath the surface, it simmered, leaving the wrath that he felt to be aimed solely at J.D. to fester, defining him. Making him less than honest. And in some ways, no better than the man he claimed to despise. Hating J.D. had become as natural to him as breathing.

On reflection, it was easy to see why the O'Sullivans disliked him.

In that moment, Jonah didn't like himself very much, either.

It would be better for everyone if he stayed away, if he left Cedar River and returned to his real life. In Portland, he knew who he was. He was civilized and successful and well liked. He had a purpose. A role to play. He wasn't an intruder. A side note to anyone's life.

In Cedar River, he felt like a fraud. A pale imitation of the man he really was.

He thought about his mother and realized it was time he let her get on with her life, too. If she loved J.D., who was he to tell her she couldn't? He really was a self-important, egotistical bastard.

And J.D. was probably fighting for his life because of him.

Because he didn't have an ounce of forgiveness in his heart. Because he blamed J.D. for everything. Because he'd done exactly what his father had accused him of—behaved like a spoiled child. Through his childhood, through his teens and then as he headed into adulthood, he'd been indulged and given every material thing he wanted. J.D. had done it to make up for his long absences;

his mother had obliged because she felt guilty. And Jonah had accepted it all with an ungracious heart. Taking, but feeling no gratitude.

Then he thought about Connie. A woman who had endured unspeakable suffering and pain and still had goodness and kindness etched into her soul. A woman whose parents barely spared her a thought and whose much-loved grandparents had passed away and left her alone. Sweet and trusting. She'd put her body and trust in his hands and he'd made a mockery of her, over and over, insisting her loyalty to the O'Sullivans—the very people who had protected her, helped her rebuild her life—was misplaced and misdirected. But what did he know about loyalty? He'd always believed he was loyal to his mother, that they were united, that their bond was unbreakable. And it was, until she did something he didn't approve of—like get involved with J.D. again. Loyalty with terms wasn't loyalty. It was blind arrogance. Something he possessed by the bucketload.

The realization made his path abundantly clear.

I need to go back to Portland. And stay there.

He needed to let his mother get on with her life. He needed to let Connie do the same.

And then, as thoughts of her bombarded his head, she appeared.

"You know," she said when she reached him, "your mom didn't mean what she said."

"I know," he said quietly.

She looked doubtful. "She's just hurting and scared."

"I know," he said again.

Connie sat down. "You need to go back in there."

He shook his head. "They don't want me around."

"It's not a matter of what they want," she said and grabbed his hands. "It's what you *need.*"

"I'm fine right here," he lied. "But you should go back."

"Not without you."

Jonah looked to where their hands were linked. "I need to stay away from them. It's better for everyone."

She blanched. "It's not better for me."

He pulled his hands away and said some of the hardest words he'd ever uttered. "I don't think I'm right for you, Connie."

She sucked in a sharp breath. "That's not true."

"The O'Sullivans mean a lot to you," he said and nodded. "And rightly so. They've protected you, helped you, made you a part of their family. But I don't belong with them, Connie. I'm not an O'Sullivan. Maybe I am by blood. But in here," he said and put a hand to his chest. "In here I'll never be one of them. And they'll never really accept me. Oh, they'll try. They'll make all the right noises and say all the right things, but it won't be real. Because my real life is in Portland. Not here."

Her eyes glistened when she realized what he meant. "You're leaving?"

"Once I know J.D. is okay, then, yes."

"What about us?"

He exhaled heavily. "You deserve someone who will fit into your life. That's not me. The O'Sullivans mean the world to you… I'll just get in the way of that."

"You're dumping me?"

They weren't nice words, but there was truth in them. "I'm ending things. Before they get too serious."

"Too serious?" she echoed. "Things *are* serious. At least they are for me. We made love. But more than that, we've become friends. You talked about marriage and—"

"I said I'd marry you if you got pregnant," he reminded her. "But marrying me would be a disaster for you, Connie. You'd always been torn between me and the O'Sullivans. I'm not criticizing you," he said when she started to protest. "In a way, I admire your loyalty. But we both know this relationship has run its course."

"How can you say something like that?" He saw her hurt and it killed him. But he was right to end it. Right to set her free.

"We've had a nice time together. But relationships don't always last, Connie. That's just how things go."

She was shaking. She was angry and hurt and he couldn't blame her. But with time, she'd see that it was better to end things now. She pushed back the chair and got to her feet.

"So, that's it?"

He nodded, aching all over. "Yeah...that's it."

Her chin came up. "I'll tell Kieran to let you know when your dad's condition is stable."

He was grateful for her concern. "Thank you."

"Goodbye, Jonah."

He said goodbye and watched her leave, feeling as though she was taking a little piece of his heart with every step away from him. He shook his head and blinked, feeling heat at the corners of his eyes. And he drew some air into his lungs, trying to erase the image of her hurt expression from his thoughts.

But it was an epic fail.

He drank more coffee, although he wasn't sure how long he sat at the table. An hour, maybe two. He was just about to get up and stretch his legs when Kieran came striding through the cafeteria and stopped by the table.

"It's not his heart," his brother said. "Looks like a severe ulcer attack."

Jonah's gut fell. "Is he going to be okay?"

Kieran nodded. "For now. His ulcers have been giving

him a lot of grief for a while now. And although he didn't have a heart attack, it's likely if he doesn't avoid stress."

"Avoid me, you mean?"

Kieran shrugged. "You should go home. Liam's with him now and I'll stop by before I head out. Don't upset him, Jonah… I don't think he could take any more stress."

Jonah watched as Kieran walked out of the cafeteria, his guilt like a weight on his shoulders. He waited for a while. A long while. And once he was sure all the O'Sullivans must have left, he made his way to the information desk, got J.D.'s room number and went to find him.

He'd been moved out of triage and was in a private room, monitors attached to him in various places. The nurse let Jonah in, offering him just a few minutes to visit. Jonah approached the bed slowly, his chest tightening even further. J.D. looked gray and very unwell. But he was alive—that was the important thing.

He stood by the bed, not moving, taking in J.D.'s closed eyes and shallow breathing, assailed by memories. Memories he'd hung on to for too long.

Connie was right. Maybe…it was time to forgive. He just had to take the first step. Even if it was the hardest thing he'd ever do. Because if he didn't do it in this moment, Jonah suspected he never would.

He took a long breath, digging deep, and then Jonah said something he hadn't dared say for close to twenty-five years.

"Dad?"

He waited, and then J.D. opened his eyes. "Hey," he croaked out. "You're here."

Jonah swallowed hard. "I'm…I'm so sorry."

J.D. patted the bed and didn't try to hide the tears in his eyes. "It's not your fault, son."

"It feels like my fault," he admitted, hearing real emotion in the way J.D. called him his son. "If I'd just let up and stopped being so—"

J.D. reached out and grabbed his hand. "It's not your fault," he said again. "My damned ulcers are acting up, that's all. Don't tell Connie or Liam, but that chef at the hotel makes the best damn fries I've ever had." He took a deep breath. "I don't want you blaming yourself. And if anyone tries to say any different, just tell them to go to hell."

Jonah grinned. "You mean Liam or Kieran?" Then he frowned. "I know they're trying. I know they are doing what they can to make the best of this situation, but the truth is, they'll never really accept me."

"They don't have to," J.D. said and sighed. "As long as you accept yourself, what does anyone else's opinion matter?"

"It matters."

J.D. sighed. "It will just take time, son. And you gotta let people in."

He had a point. But Jonah still knew what he had to do. "Things will be better if I go back to Portland."

"Running away doesn't solve anything."

"I know," he said quietly. "But I'm not running. I'm just going back to my real life. But I wanted to say… about you and Mom… I'm okay with it."

"I'm glad. She cares about what you think. You're the most important thing in the world to her, you know."

Jonah did know. "She always put me first. Now I think it's time she put herself first. That's why I'm leaving… to give you two a chance to make it work without Mom thinking I'm being all disapproving and resentful. Just treat her right."

"I will," J.D. promised. "And thanks for calling me

Dad. It means the world to me." He paused. "So, what about Connie?"

"I ended it."

"You sure that's what you want to do?"

"Yes," he replied, dying inside. "It's for the best. She deserves better than me."

"Don't underestimate yourself, son," J.D. said quietly and earnestly. "You're a good man. Your mom, she raised you right."

Jonah squeezed his father's hand.

"You both raised me right," he said, and realized they were probably the kindest words he could've said to the older man. And in a way, the forgiveness J.D. had been seeking. He knew he had a long way to go—but it was a start.

He waited for a few seconds, saw his father's lids close and then turned on his heel, shocked to see his mother standing in the doorway. She looked distraught, as though her world was falling apart, and Jonah knew he'd played a leading role in making her unhappy.

When he reached her, he took a long breath and nodded. "I think he'll be okay."

Kathleen reached out and grasped his arm, holding him steady. "What I said earlier… I shouldn't have said that in front of everyone and—"

"It's fine, Mom," he assured her gently. "I think I needed to hear it."

There were tears in her eyes, and Jonah realized all he'd done in the past few hours was hurt the people he cared about most in the world. "I was scared and—"

"I know," he said and grasped her hand. "Don't worry about it, Mom. Just take care of yourself. I want you to be happy," he said and sighed. "And if J.D. makes you happy, I'm not going to make things difficult for you."

Tears fell down her cheeks. "We both love you very much."

His throat constricted. "I know."

"And Connie loves you, too," she said quietly. "Don't throw it away."

Jonah's eyes burned. Connie loved him? He wasn't so sure. They were lovers. Friends. But they hadn't said the words. Jonah wasn't sure he had the courage to love anyone…to be vulnerable…to be completely open to another human being. He'd watched his mother love J.D. for thirty years and get nothing in return. It had made him cynical. And, yeah…afraid.

"She's been through so much," he said rawly, unsure if his mother knew about Connie's past, and then saw compassion in her expression and realized that she did. "And she deserves more than my messed-up life. She's close to the O'Sullivans, and rightly so. If I'm around, I'll just get in the way of that."

"Who says she can't have both?"

"Me. Not when I feel about them the way I do. I *can* make peace with J.D., and I can accept that you two are together, but the rest of them…" His words trailed off for a moment. "They want to make me fit into their nice little family unit, and I can't. I'm not one of them. I'm a Rickard, Mom, not an O'Sullivan. You know that as much as I do."

"Who says you can't be both?"

"I do," he replied heavily. "I know myself. I don't want to be a part of them, knowing it's just because they feel they have to include me, for J.D.'s sake. They don't really like me, and that's fine, I can live with that. I don't need them," he said, hating that the words made him feel so foolishly alone. "But Connie does. And I won't ask her to choose. They were there for her when she was young, when she needed protection. I wasn't."

"You can't slay her dragons, Jonah," his mother said, as though reading his mind. "And you can't change the past. You have to live for today and hope for tomorrow."

"I know, Mom," he said and hugged her briefly. "But Connie needs them more than she needs me in her life."

"What she needs," his mother said pointedly, "is your love. Don't forget that in your desire to do the right thing, or be honorable, or in thinking that she would choose loyalty over anything else."

"I know her," he said and tapped his chest. "I know this is for the best."

As he said goodbye and walked away, Jonah realized that he was totally in love with Connie. And that's why he was letting her go.

Four days into her new job as assistant manager of the O'Sullivan Hotel, Connie knew that the longer hours and busy schedule were exactly what she needed to keep from going out of her mind. Christmas was looming, and she had already handled more than one potential mishap. The sous chef quit, for starters, over a dispute with the head chef, and it took all of Connie's negotiating skills to get the two to work out their differences.

If only it had been that easy between her and Jonah!

She hadn't heard from him. She hadn't heard his voice or his laugh or a whisper against her skin as they made love. Nothing. Nada. Zilch. It was as though he'd dropped off the face of the planet. Which, of course, he hadn't. He was back in Portland. Back where he belonged.

And she missed him.

She missed him so much she ached inside.

But she wasn't about to call him. He was the one who'd

ended things. He was the one who didn't think they were worth fighting for. Worth anything, really. To Jonah, she was clearly just someone who had warmed his bed a few times. Warmed *her* bed, actually. Since their relationship had played out mostly in the confines of her house. Which meant every room was filled with memories of him... *of them*. As brief as it had been, Jonah was her first real relationship...the first man she'd allowed into her bed and her heart. And now both those things felt empty.

"Connie?"

Liam had poked his head in the door. She looked up from her desk.

"Are you coming?" he asked.

She nodded. He'd invited her to dinner with his family, a kind of pre-Christmas catch-up, all the more important because J.D. was back on his feet and Sean had arrived a couple of days earlier from Los Angeles to see the family over the holiday season.

"Sure," she said and packed up her desk.

The restaurant was busy, but a corner table had been reserved and everyone was there.

Not everyone.

J.D. and Kathleen were out and about together. All of the O'Sullivans and the Rickards had shown up, even Gwen, who had clearly and graciously come to terms with her ex-husband's relationship with Kathleen. It was a noisy group. Nicola's two nephews were chatting tirelessly, Gwen and J.D.'s three young granddaughters were keeping the older woman occupied. Everyone who was an O'Sullivan, either by birth or marriage or some other link, was there.

Except Jonah.

His absence was conspicuous. At least to Connie. Somehow, she found herself seated between J.D. and

Liam, and she thought how poignant that was. Ten years ago, both men had saved her. Not only from her attackers, but from pain and humiliation. They'd protected her, watched over her, given her hope and opportunity. And she'd grown strong under their protection.

But as she sipped wine and made small talk, Connie experienced an acute sense of disconnect. Not that she would allow anyone to see it. No one except Jonah. She had let him into her life and her heart, unlike she ever had before. Past her walls, to truly see her. And he listened. He was the most wonderful listener. And now, she missed that.

Looking around, she knew that they felt sorry for her, or commiserated with her, or thought she was better off without him. Or all three things. And there had been times since he'd left when she was torn between loving and hating him. But loving always won out.

"Everything okay Connie?"

It was J.D., looking healthier and more robust than he had in ages. It was wonderful to see him so happy and content and clearly in love with Kathleen. Everyone seemed happy.

Everyone except me.

"I'm fine," she lied and plastered on a smile.

"New job going well?"

She nodded. "Perfectly. Liam's only slightly less bossy than usual."

"I heard that," Liam said and grinned. "Don't be fooled—Connie rules the hotel, not me. I'm thrilled to take a step back and let someone else be the boss some of the time."

"Me, too," Kayla said and sighed lovingly when Liam

grasped her hand. "I love that we get to spend more time at home with Jack. Together."

Yeah, there certainly was a lot of couple love at the table. Other than Gwen, who was wrapped up in her granddaughters, only Sean looked slightly out of place. But he appeared more bored than anything else. And Connie's loneliness amplified tenfold.

"I miss him," she whispered, unsure if anyone heard.

J.D. did. So did Kathleen.

His mother sighed. "Me, too. He's just so distant these days."

"Well," the older man said, "he has to work this out in his own way and his own time."

Connie wasn't so sure. Jonah was stubborn. And opinionated. But he was also incredibly emotional and breathtakingly passionate. Not really traits of someone who thrived on isolation. She didn't believe that about him. He loved his mother, and as much as he'd denied it, she knew he cared about J.D. Plus, she'd watched him around his brothers; she'd seen firsthand the budding camaraderie and friendship. But it was early days. Too early for Jonah. He was so stubborn, and so afraid of being hurt, she knew he couldn't see an end to the whole complicated situation. But there was, she was sure of it. He just had to open himself up to it. Stubbornness, she thought again. He was cloaked in the stuff.

"He's a jerk," Liam said quietly but impatiently. "Forget about him."

Connie turned her attention to her boss. "I can't. Can you?"

He shrugged. "Dad's right…he needs to work this out for himself. Forcing him to accept us isn't his style."

They didn't know him at all.

"It's about self-preservation," she said, louder this time. "Do any of you think you'd behave any differently if the roles had been reversed?"

Eight sets of eyes, excluding the kids', zoomed in on her. Everyone thought they knew him. But they'd only scratched the surface. No one understood. Except perhaps Kathleen.

And Gwen.

From the end of the table, Gwen was nodding. "Connie's right. Everyone is quick to judge, but take a moment to consider how you would feel, being faced with this group. I like Jonah," she said and smiled at Connie. "And I think he's exactly what this family needs. Someone who isn't bogged down in our reputation or social standing. Someone who sees us all for what we are— flawed and imperfect and full of love for one another, even if it's *hard* to love each other sometimes. You think he needs space?" Gwen said and shook her head. "What he needs is exactly the opposite. He needs to know that we're *not* okay with him keeping his distance."

Connie's heart almost burst with pride and admiration for the other woman.

Because Gwen was right.

Jonah didn't need space…he'd *had* space for thirty years.

"Thank you, Gwen. You're right. That's exactly what he needs." She got to her feet. "If you'll excuse me."

"Where are you going?" J.D. asked, clearly concerned.

Connie took a breath and looked around the table. She cared about these people. All of them in different ways. But it was Jonah she loved. Jonah she wanted. Jonah she needed.

"I'm going to Portland," she announced, her resolve and determination growing with each passing second.

"And even if I have drag Jonah back by the ankles, kicking and screaming," she said, and smiled, suddenly so ridiculously happy she wanted to sing, "I'm going to bring him home."

Chapter Twelve

Jonah moped around the apartment on Saturday afternoon, thinking about how much time he'd spent *thinking* lately. He wished he was a drinker or had some other sort of meaningful vice. But he was barely a social drinker and had quit smoking after the first puff on a cigarette when he was fifteen.

He toyed with the idea of catching up with friends, but he really wasn't in the mood for small talk. And since it had been raining nonstop for the past two days, it was as good an excuse as any to stay indoors and mope. The holidays were coming, and he figured he needed to think about his plans. He'd deliberately put off talking to his mother about it, because he knew what she wanted. Her family. Together.

But he wasn't ready for it. He was still coming to terms with forgiving his father.

And falling in love with Connie.

And then letting her go.

Even if his head told him it was for the best, Jonah ached inside, missing her so much he spent his time working and sleeping and little else. He hadn't called her, hadn't sent a text message, hadn't asked about her when he spoke to his mother a week earlier. A clean break was best.

But he missed her. He missed her sweet touch. Her kiss. The scent she wore that was uniquely hers. He missed the gentle sound of her voice. And he missed her friendship. He missed knowing she could read him without saying a word. That she could get so far under his skin they could share a mere look and understand one another.

He'd never believed in soul mates. He'd always thought it to be nonsense, something invented to fuel the imaginations of sappy, sentimental people.

But now, he wasn't so sure. Because Connie had reached him—soul deep—and he had no hope of getting her out of his heart. Only time would make things easier. But time had become notoriously slow. The days dragged and the nights were worse.

He sighed and was about to watch television for a while when the doorbell buzzed. He wasn't expecting anyone and figured it must be one of the neighbors.

But it wasn't.

It was Connie standing on his doorstep, drenched from the rain, her blond hair plastered to her head, wearing a completely unsuitable wool coat over jeans and a sweater.

He stared at her, as though his feet were entrenched in cement, unable to move for a moment as he absorbed the sight of her. Until he realized she was shivering and he grabbed her arm, hauling her gently across the threshold.

"What are you doing?" he demanded and began to tug off her coat. "Trying to catch pneumonia?"

Her teeth chattered. "I forgot to pack a raincoat."

He stripped the coat off and dropped it on the floor and he closed the door. "How did you get past the security gate?"

"Your mom told me the code," she explained, shivering. "And your address."

Jonah stared at her—bedraggled, chilled to the bone, her mascara running and still totally beautiful. He made a mental note to have a word with his mother for not forewarning him and shook his head. "What are you doing here?"

"You invited me," she reminded him. "Remember? You said you wanted me to see your city."

"That was before—"

"Before you dumped me," she said, teeth still chattering. "I remember."

Jonah winced. "That's not what I meant. I'm just surprised to see you."

She shivered and he grabbed her hand. "You need to get warm and out of those wet things. Come with me."

He walked her upstairs to his bedroom and ushered her into the bathroom.

"My overnight bag is in my rental car," she said as he pulled a pair of sweatpants and a fleece shirt from a drawer.

"I'll get your bag later," he said and dropped the clothes onto the bed. "Take a hot shower and get changed. I'll make you some tea."

He left the room to give her some privacy and headed back downstairs.

And for the next twenty minutes, he overthought every possible scenario as to why she'd landed on his doorstep so unexpectedly.

J.D. had suffered a relapse.

She was pregnant.

She couldn't live without him.

None of his mental ranting made sense. J.D. was fine—his mother had said as much. Of course she could live without him—it wasn't as though they'd been together very long. Sure, they'd had a real connection and some incredible sex. But it wasn't enough to sustain feelings long-term.

Even if he missed her like crazy.

So, maybe she was pregnant. That had to be the reason she was in his apartment.

"That's better," she said when she appeared in the kitchen looking warm and dry, other than her still damp hair. "I wasn't expecting so much rain. I should have checked my weather app."

His spine twitched. "Tea?"

She nodded and smiled. "It's good to see you."

He avoided a smile. She had some serious explaining to do. "Why are you here, Connie?"

"Why do you think?"

Jonah stopped making the tea and came around the counter. "Are you pregnant?" he asked, figuring he should get the hard question out of the way first.

"No," she said and shook her head. "I'm sorry to say."

He rocked back on his heels. She sounded disappointed. "What are you saying? You want to have a baby?"

"At some point," she replied. "I'd like very much to have a child."

He swallowed. "With me?"

"With you," she said.

"Why?"

She shuddered, took a breath and then sighed. "Because I'm in love with you."

The world stopped spinning. That was the only reason there could be for the way his whole body seemed to sway and then float as though there was no gravity beneath his feet.

"Why?" he asked again, stupidly.

"Because…I am. I don't know how or why. It just happened. That's how it goes, Jonah, when people fall in love…it just happens."

"I'm not exactly lovable." He wasn't sure what to say. She was opening a door for him—and he wanted so much to walk through. But letting go of old fears was harder than he'd ever imagined.

She smiled and his heart raced. "You are to me. And you are to your mom and your dad. And even your brothers."

"They think I'm responsible for J.D.'s collapse," he reminded her. "And they're right. I am. I can't imagine they'll be warming to me anytime soon."

"Well, they won't get a chance if you don't talk to them."

He shrugged. He knew what she was saying, what she was asking. But it was better for everyone if he stayed away. "I'm happy here."

"You're a terrible liar."

"Would you rather I tell you things that aren't true?" he shot back. "That's not my style."

"I know that," she said quietly. "It's one of the reasons why I love you."

"Would you stop saying that?" he said, harsher than he liked, confused and torn and his mind utterly blown by her confession.

She shook her head. "I came here to tell you that I love you," she said, her voice raw.

Jonah's insides ached. "I'm no good for you, Connie."

"Would you stop saying that?" she said, echoing his

words from seconds earlier, moving closer until she stood in front of him.

Jonah clenched. "Are you planning on seducing me?"

"If it will give me an edge."

He sighed. "Sex won't change anything."

"No," she said and touched his chest. "But I love the way you make love to me. And I fall a little bit more in love with you every time you touch me."

They were inflammatory words. Honest words. More than he could stand.

So he kissed her. Because it had been a long two weeks since he'd felt the sweetness of her mouth against his own, and he needed her kiss like he needed air to breathe.

They moved to the sofa, since he was certain his legs wouldn't make it to the bedroom. And they made love, hotter than he'd known it, wilder, with more urgency and passion than he'd believed possible. Jonah held on to her as she shuddered beneath him and then, when he couldn't hold back any longer, he let himself go to that place of sweet oblivion.

They lay together, panting, coming slowly back down to earth. Afterward, he drew her into his arms and carried her to the bedroom. They slept for a while, and later made love again. When they stirred it was past seven o'clock. He retrieved her overnight bag from her rental car, then ordered a pizza and opened a bottle of wine, and by nine they were on the sofa, not talking, just sipping wine and clearly aware of the uncomfortable silence brewing between them.

Finally, she spoke. "Your mom misses you. She said you haven't committed to seeing her over the holidays."

Jonah rubbed her bare calf, thinking how sexy she looked in one of his sweaters, her lovely legs entwined with his. "I have a lot of work to do."

"I told your family I would bring you back, kicking and screaming if I had to," she announced, watching him over the rim of her glass. "They all thought it was a great idea."

He laughed humorlessly. "I think we've already established that I don't belong in Cedar River."

"Of course you do," she said. "Whether you want to admit it or not, Cedar River is your home, Jonah. Your mom and dad are there. Your family is there."

You're there...

Logically, she made complete sense...because for the last two weeks, Portland had felt less and less like home. But he'd made his decision and intended to stick to it.

"I'm not going back," he said flatly.

"Stubborn jerk," she said and swung her legs off the bed. "You don't deserve my love."

"I know that."

She got to her feet and pulled the sweater down over her thighs. "If you don't come back, I don't ever want to see you again."

"Okay."

Her face blotched with color. "Really? That's it?"

"What do you want from me, Connie?" he implored and stood, hands on hips. "I told you how it was two weeks ago."

"You were hurting and I thought you needed some time to come to your senses. We all did. But now you've had time and you need to come home."

"This is my home, Connie. Whatever else you think, it's all in your imagination."

Her stare turned into a glare. "Then why did you make love to me just now? Why didn't you turn me away when I arrived?"

"Because I'm crazy for you," he rasped. "You know that."

Her eyes sparked. "You love me?"

"That's not what I said," he replied, backpedaling. Admitting he loved her wasn't going to help defuse the situation. Better she thought he didn't. "Don't overreact."

"So, it's just sex?"

"That's not what I said, either. But unless you're willing to move here with me, I don't see how we can have a future." He sighed heavily. "I don't want to hurt you, Connie. But I won't make empty promises, either…that's not who I am. I can't move to a small town and be a part of the great O'Sullivan legacy. And whether you want to admit it, or not, you *are* a part of that legacy. They adore you, and rightly so. You're like the glue they all need. And you need them. I get that. And I would never ask you to let go of that connection. It's a part of who you are. It *makes* you who you are. The reality is, they're more your family than they will ever be mine."

"And you don't want them?"

"Exactly."

"But they want you."

"For now," he said, frustrated and confused. "Until the novelty wears off. And it will. Right now they think they're doing me a favor by trying to include me in their inner circle and then act as though I should be honored or humbled or feel some other damned thing. But I don't, and that's why they keep pushing. Because people like the O'Sullivans always have to win. Well," he said harshly, "I'm not some prize, consolation or otherwise."

She took a moment to reply, searching his face with her eyes. "And that's how you really feel?"

"Yes."

"You're wrong about them. They're trying to include you because you are a part of their family."

"It's pity," he said flatly. "Nothing more."

She nodded wearily. "Okay. I guess we have nothing else to say to one another. I'll get dressed and leave."

"You can stay. I'll sleep down here—you take my room."

She didn't argue. Didn't resist. She didn't say another word.

Once she was out of sight, he slumped onto the sofa and put his head in his hands. He really wished he'd never heard of Cedar River. Or the O'Sullivans. Or Connie Bedford.

Because he couldn't remember ever being more miserable in his life.

He closed his eyes and begged his weary brain not to dream. And failed.

When he awoke the next morning, he was alone. And he wasn't surprised.

But there was a note propped up on the counter in the kitchen. He stared at the thing for close to half an hour. Because he didn't want to read her goodbye, even though he'd told her they were done.

Dear Jonah.

A decade ago, I needed someone to take my hand and say, here...take control back. And I did. I worked hard to forget that awful time in my life and become a whole and functional person, someone I could be proud of. And then I met you, and you flipped a switch inside me. A light I didn't know I possessed. I felt real passion and somehow I reclaimed what had been taken from me. With you, I wasn't afraid. Maybe because, underneath your arrogance, I saw my fear reflected in you and I realized I wasn't alone.

I know you think the O'Sullivans want to control you, but really, it's the other way around. You've always known about them, and you've always chosen to stay away and remain hidden in the shadows. That's a power they didn't have, because up until eleven months ago, they didn't know you existed. But now they do know, and it scares you to death. But you have a chance to change things, to bring everyone together, to have the family you've always wanted. All you need to do is forgive and move forward. I know you have the strength to do that. I just wish you could see yourself as I do.

Love, Connie.

Jonah stared at the note for a long time after he'd read it. And felt the truth of her words right down to the marrow in his bones. He'd never really considered himself to be in control of anything—or anyone. Determined, yes. Arrogant…well, yeah. But looking at her note, Jonah saw his reflection and it shamed him, deep down.

You've always chosen to stay away and remain hidden in the shadows.

Because that's exactly what he had done. Stayed in control by staying silent. When the truth was, he could have confronted J.D. and demanded the truth come out years ago. But by remaining a secret, he'd *had* control. And he'd let that feed his bitterness. His rage. His resentment.

My way or the highway.

His brother had said that.

And Connie, the most courageous person he had ever met, had called him out on his arrogant belief that he could do exactly as he pleased and not give a hoot how it affected everyone else. He'd told his mother he was giving her space to continue her relationship with J.D., when the truth was, instead of supporting her by *being* there, he'd bailed.

And there was Connie. Who was the best thing that had ever happened to him.

His lover. His friend. Perhaps the best he'd ever had. A woman who had somehow, despite his appalling behavior, managed to see enough of the man he really was and still find a way to love him.

Jonah got to his feet and looked around. Nothing about the apartment comforted him. Nothing felt right.

What the hell are you doing, Rickard?

He inhaled. Exhaled. And made a decision.

I'm going home.

Connie was neck-deep in training Liam's new PA on Wednesday morning when Liam called to ask her to tend to a disgruntled customer at the concierge desk.

But when she got there, the concierge was looking at her oddly and Liam was standing in the center of the foyer. So was J.D. And Kathleen. And Kieran. And Gwen. They were standing close together, so she headed for them but halted the moment she spotted Jonah in the middle of their circle.

Ten feet away, and four days since she'd been so close to him, she still wasn't sure whether she loved him or hated him. He'd let her go—twice. He really didn't deserve any more chances. But she wasn't going to jump to any conclusions. He was obviously in town to see his parents. She wasn't exactly keeping track of his movements. He'd made his thoughts abundantly clear.

They were over.

She looked at Liam and frowned.

"Sorry, Connie," he said and shrugged. "I couldn't say no. He's my brother, after all."

Connie didn't have a clue what was happening. She glared at Jonah, hands on hips. "What are you doing?"

He took a breath, and she noticed he looked edgy. "Letting go."

She frowned, glanced at J.D. and Kathleen and noticed they were holding hands and nodding reassuringly. "Letting go of what?" she demanded.

He took a step closer to her. "Control."

Her heart skipped a beat. What did that mean? "You're not making sense, and I really don't want to make a scene here in the hotel foyer."

"I need to say something," he said, swallowing convulsively. "To you. Right now."

Connie stayed still…and waited.

"I met you in this hotel eleven months ago," he said quietly. "And I behaved badly. So I'd like to go back to that day and start over." He took a long breath, almost as though it was the hardest he'd ever inhaled. "Hi…my name is Jonah. I'm thirty years old and I'm an architect. My mother's name is Kathleen, my father's name is J.D. I have three older brothers and a sister who tragically passed away a few years ago. I also have several nieces and nephews, and I'm pretty sure there'll be more of those on the way at some point. My whole family lives in Cedar River," he said, his voice cracking. "It's a nice town…a good place to settle down, get married, have a family."

Connie eyes heated instantly. "Jonah… I…"

"I'm in love with you, Connie."

His words were the sweetest she had ever heard. And probably the hardest he had ever said. And he'd said them in a public place, with his family watching. *His family.*

Public acknowledgment. There was no going back from that. She moved over to him, reached up to touch his face and kissed him.

"I love you, too," she whispered and then his arms were around her.

From the corner of her eye, she saw Liam smiling, saw him and the rest of the family huddled close, and everyone was clearly delighted. Then she only saw Jonah. So strong and familiar. Everything she wanted.

"I need to ask you a question," he said against her mouth.

Connie heart soared. "Not here. Let's go upstairs."

"Good," he said and laughed softly. "I think I've made a big enough fool out of myself today. You know I'm never going to hear the end of this from my brothers, don't you?"

"They came to support you?"

He nodded. "I needed all the help I can get."

She grabbed his hand turned to his family. "We'll be in my office."

They all laughed and headed for the restaurant, and Connie quickly forgot all about them as she and Jonah took the elevator upstairs. One they were in her office, she closed the door and pressed her back against it.

"I got your note," he said and smiled.

"I might have gotten a little carried away that night," she said and made no protest when he led her to the sofa by the window. "It was either write a note or cry myself to sleep."

He winced. "I'm so sorry. The last thing I ever want to do is make you cry."

She fought back tears. "You said you loved me."

"Get used to that," he said and drew her closer. "I do love you, more than I can say."

"Oh, I don't know," she teased. "I think you say it pretty well. But you also said you had to ask me a question."

"I do," he said and grasped her hands tightly in his. "Do I need to get on one knee for this? What's the modern-day protocol? I've never done this before."

She laughed happily. "No knees required," she assured him. "The hand-holding is all I need."

He grinned and pulled a small box from his jacket with his free hand. Then he took a long and unsteady breath. "Connie Bedford…will you marry me?"

Her heart expanded again, and she experienced an intense surge of joy. "Yes. Yes. Yes."

He laughed and flipped open the box, revealing a beautiful diamond solitaire. "So, I take it that's a yes?"

She flung herself against him and accepted his kiss. And his ring. It fit perfectly.

"It's so beautiful."

"You're beautiful," he said and held her. "Inside and out."

"What made you change your—"

"You," he said, cutting her off. "Your note. Realizing that you came to Portland even though I'd been stupid enough to let you go once. You are gutsy and strong and I am humbled that you love me, Connie. Honestly, I can't believe my luck."

"It's not luck," she said and melted. "You are the most amazing man I have ever met."

He looked skeptical. "Hmm. Arrogant. Opinionated. Judgmental. I've called you a fool. A doormat. A—"

"Okay," she said and waved a hand. "I get the picture. You have been a jerk. But in a way, you were right. I think until I met you, I did let people take advantage of me a little."

"People?"

She sighed. "Okay… Liam. And maybe J.D. But not in a bad way."

"I know," he assured her gently. "I know Liam and my dad care about you."

"Dad?"

He shrugged and smiled ruefully. "I gave up the fight."

"I'm so glad. And immensely proud. It took a lot of courage."

"No," he said, kissing her cheek. "You're the courageous one. And it probably takes a whole lot of courage to love me."

"Not at all."

She smiled, so happy she was ready to burst. "So, where are we going to live? Portland?"

"Not a chance," he replied and grinned. "You're here. That's where I want to be."

She laughed and then said more soberly, "But your career? How will you—"

"We'll work something out," he promised. "And truthfully, I want to be here, in Cedar River. I want us to raise our kids here."

"Kids?"

His brows shot up. "Isn't that part of this deal?"

"You bet. Want to start practicing?"

He laughed. "Absolutely, Miss Bedford."

And then he kissed her.

Epilogue

"How are you holding up?"

Jonah looked at his father, dressed in a suit almost identical to the one he wore, a small flower in the lapel. "I'm okay. You?"

J.D. grinned broadly. "Great. Never better. Today's a good day."

Jonah nodded. "Who would have thought?"

"Sometimes the planets align just long enough for us to make the smart decisions."

"Have you been reading Mom's astrology books or something?" he teased and laughed.

"The things a man will do for love."

Jonah laughed again. His father was right. He'd made a few big decisions in the past four months. Quitting his job in Portland. Joining a small but progressive firm in Rapid City. Selling his apartment. Buying a house half-way between that town and Cedar River so they could both commute, with a big yard for her dogs. And several rooms that would hopefully one day be occupied by their children. Connie had made it very clear she wanted more than one, and he was only too happy to oblige.

Yeah…his life certainly had changed.

But Jonah wouldn't have it any other way.

He would give Connie the moon and the stars if he could. Thankfully, she insisted she was content with his love and devotion.

"I'm really proud of you," J.D. said and hugged him.

Jonah didn't resist. His resisting days were over. It had been a long road. One fraught with rage and bitterness and one that left him with more than a few regrets. But over time, he was sure, the regrets would fade.

"When you two decide to stop hugging," Liam said from the doorway, "you might want to remember that we have a wedding to get to."

Jonah pulled back and laughed. He didn't mind Liam so much these days. His oldest brother was still a pain in the ass, but he was also a good and honorable man. The kind of man Jonah wanted as a friend as well as a brother. And he liked Kieran a lot. Sean was still pretty cold, but maybe he'd mellow down the road.

The ceremony was taking place in a small chapel in town, and the reception was at the hotel. Nothing too fancy, just as the bride had insisted. Jonah grabbed his keys and straightened his jacket, noticing that J.D. was lingering by the window.

"Dad," he said, the word now part of his vocabulary. "You coming?"

J.D. smiled, moisture plumping in the crinkles at the corner of his eyes. "Absolutely."

They walked out together and met Kieran and Sean in the hallway—they were dressed in the same penguin suits, sans ties. The drive to the chapel in Liam's Silverado was filled with laughter and dissing and a closeness Jonah had come to value more than he'd believed possible.

The white chapel, with its tall steeple and wide-open doors, was welcoming and filled with about thirty close friends and family. Jonah stood by the altar, his father at his side, and he noticed J.D. was tugging at his collar. Music started, an old instrumental number that made him smile.

Until he spotted Connie by the doors. She began walking down the aisle, her gaze connected to his. She looked so beautiful in her shell-pink gown, flowers crowning her head, the smile on her face only for him. Every ounce of love he felt for her rose up and hit him squarely in the chest. She arrived at the altar, taking her place, and then their attention moved back toward the rear of the church.

The bride had arrived.

Jonah had never seen his mother look more beautiful. In her ivory lace gown and short veil she was a vision, glowing with joy and love for the man she was about to take as her husband.

His parents were getting married.

It was up there as one of the happiest moments of his life.

Connie really did love weddings. And this one more than any other she'd ever been a part of or helped organize. Kathleen truly was a dream bride, and she had never seen a more devoted groom than J.D.

The reception was going off without a hitch. There had a been a few speeches, one from J.D., who had an obvious tear in his eyes when spoke about his bride. Liam had made his own speech, and then Jonah had spoken about his parents with such heartfelt respect and affection, she couldn't have been prouder.

By the time the cake was cut and the dancing started, more than a few tears had been shed.

"Hey," Jonah said and came up behind her, wrapping a protective arm around her waist. "Have I mentioned how beautiful you look?"

Connie turned in his arms. "Once or twice. You don't look so bad yourself. And your mom looks so lovely. She made such a beautiful bride."

"So will you," he said and kissed the corner of her mouth.

Their wedding was planned for the summer, giving Connie plenty of time to plan and make the day as memorable as possible. The ring on her finger sparkled, and she experienced an acute and consuming wave of love for the man in front of her.

The past few months had been a whirlwind. Jonah had moved his life to South Dakota, Connie was loving her new job and once the wedding was over, she planned on getting serious about making a baby with her new husband.

"I think you owe me a dance, Mr. Rickard."

"I believe I do, Miss Bedford," he said and smiled as he twirled her around, leading her to the dance floor.

Once she was in his arms, Connie relaxed against him. "Do you remember the last time we danced at a wedding?"

"You stepped on my toe."

"I did not!"

He chuckled. "You did."

"You were mean to me," she reminded him cheekily.

"But you saw right through me," he said, nuzzling her jaw discreetly. "You did from the moment we met."

She shrugged. "I knew you were mush under that moody exterior."

He smiled warmly. "You know, I've been thinking about the whole Rickard versus O'Sullivan thing. Once we have a baby, the names might be confusing…so I was thinking that maybe it's time I…" His voice trailed off and she sensed he was very uncomfortable about what he was saying.

So she helped him. "You want to change your name?"

He shrugged. "I don't know… I was only thinking."

"You could," she said tactfully. "But don't do it for anyone but yourself. You are who you are. The name you go by doesn't change that. I will take whatever name you have… Rickard or O'Sullivan. It's you I love…not your name."

He held her tight. "I love you, Connie. You're the best person I have ever known. I'm so glad you're going to marry me."

Her insides clenched. "I'm glad, too. I can't wait."

"Not long now," he reminded her.

"So much has changed," she remarked, swaying against him, oblivious to everyone and everything else in the room.

"Change is good," he affirmed. "Look at my parents."

She held him tightly. "I'm so proud of you for making peace with your dad. They love you."

"I love them," he replied. "Both of them. I'm even starting to get used to having brothers. And if it wasn't for you, I don't think I would ever have been able to admit that. You make me a better man, Connie. And I am truly humbled that you are going to be at my side for the rest of my life."

"I wouldn't want to be anywhere else," she said on a sigh, loving his strength and his integrity. "And maybe later," she said and wound her hands up his shoulders, "we could go home and practice some more of that baby making."

He kissed her deeply, getting good-natured catcalls from Liam and Kieran. "It's a date."

Connie smiled, loving him and knowing she had everything she had ever dreamed of.

And more.

* * * * *

COMING SOON!

We really hope you enjoyed reading this book. If you're looking for more romance, be sure to head to the shops when new books are available on

Thursday
26th July

MILLS & BOON

Coming next month

CARRYING THE BILLIONAIRE'S BABY
Susan Meier

'Go ahead. Just lay your hands on either side.'

He gingerly laid one hand on her T-shirt-covered baby
bump.

She reached down and took his other hand and brought
it to her stomach too. 'We may have to wait a few
seconds…oops. No. There he is.' She laughed. 'Or she.'

Jake laughed nervously. 'Oh, my goodness.'

'Feeling that makes it real, doesn't it?'

'Yes.'

His voice was hoarse, so soft that she barely heard
him. They had a mere three weeks of dating, but she
knew that tone. His voice had gotten that way only one
other time—the first time he'd seen her naked.

Something inside her cracked just a little bit. Her
pride. He might be a stuffy aristocrat, but there was a
part of him that was a normal man. And she had to play
fair.

The baby kicked again, and she stayed right where
she was. 'Ask me anything. I can see you're dying to
know.'

He smoothed his hands along her T-shirt as if memo-
rising the shape of her belly. 'I'm not even sure what
to ask.'

'There's not a lot to tell. You already know I had

morning sickness. At the end of a long day, I'm usually exhausted. But as far as the baby is concerned, this—' she motioned to her tummy '—feeling him move—is as good as it gets.'

'I care about all of it, you know.'

'All of what?'

'Not just the baby. You. I know you want to stay sharp in your profession, so you don't want to quit your job, but...really... Avery. If you'd let me, you'd never have to work another day in your life.'

She studied him. This time the offer of money wasn't condescending or out of place. It was his reaction to touching his child, albeit through her skin.

Continue reading
CARRYING THE BILLIONAIRE'S BABY
Susan Meier

Available next month
www.millsandboon.co.uk

LET'S TALK
Romance

For exclusive extracts, competitions
and special offers, find us online: